山有扶苏

美得窒息的诗经

许渊冲 译　闫红 解析

汉英对照

长江出版传媒
长江文艺出版社

目录

Contents

一 云谁之思

周南·葛覃 …… 02
周南·螽斯 …… 04
召南·采蘩 …… 06
召南·行露 …… 08
召南·何彼襛矣 …… 10
邶风·简兮 …… 12
邶风·柏丹 …… 14
邶风·桑中 …… 16
鄘风·蝃蝀 …… 18
鄘风·相鼠 …… 20
鄘风·干旄 …… 22
鄘风·芄兰 …… 24
卫风·伯兮 …… 26
卫风·黍离 …… 28
王风·扬之水 …… 30
王风·丘中有麻 …… 32
郑风·缁衣 …… 34
郑风·蘀兮 …… 36
郑风·丰 …… 38
郑风·溱洧 …… 40

二 清扬婉兮

齐风·还 …… 44
齐风·著 …… 46
齐风·东方之日 …… 48
齐风·甫田 …… 50
齐风·猗嗟 …… 52
魏风·葛屦 …… 54
魏风·十亩之间 …… 56
唐风·扬之水 …… 58
唐风·采苓 …… 60
秦风·小戎 …… 62
秦风·渭阳 …… 66
秦风·权舆 …… 68
陈风·墓门 …… 70
桧风·羔裘 …… 72
桧风·隰有苌楚 …… 74
曹风·候人 …… 76
曹风·鸤鸠 …… 78
豳风·伐柯 …… 82
豳风·九罭 …… 84
豳风·狼跋 …… 86

谷风之什·小明 …… 148
谷风之什·鼓钟 …… 152
谷风之什·信南山 …… 154
甫田之什·甫田 …… 158
甫田之什·大田 …… 162
甫田之什·瞻彼洛矣 …… 166
甫田之什·桑扈 …… 168
鱼藻之什·鱼藻 …… 170
鱼藻之什·都人士 …… 172
鱼藻之什·白华 …… 176
鱼藻之什·绵蛮 …… 180
鱼藻之什·渐渐之石 …… 184
鱼藻之什·何草不黄 …… 186

五 …… 维天之命

清庙之什·清庙 …… 276
清庙之什·维天之命 …… 278
清庙之什·维清 …… 280
清庙之什·烈文 …… 282
清庙之什·天作 …… 284
臣工之什·臣工 …… 286
臣工之什·噫嘻 …… 288
臣工之什·振鹭 …… 290
臣工之什·丰年 …… 292
臣工之什·有瞽 …… 294
臣工之什·潜 …… 296
闵予小子之什·闵予小子 …… 298
闵予小子之什·访落 …… 300
闵予小子之什·敬之 …… 302
闵予小子之什·小毖 …… 304
闵予小子之什·载芟 …… 306
闵予小子之什·良耜 …… 310

三 幽幽南山

鹿鸣之什·伐木 …… 90
鹿鸣之什·出车 …… 95
鹿鸣之什·杕杜 …… 98
南有嘉鱼之什·南有嘉鱼 …… 102
南有嘉鱼之什·南山有台 …… 104
南有嘉鱼之什·菁菁者莪 …… 108
南有嘉鱼之什·六月 …… 111
南有嘉鱼之什·吉日 …… 114
鸿雁之什·鸿雁 …… 116
鸿雁之什·沔水 …… 118
鸿雁之什·鹤鸣 …… 120
鸿雁之什·白驹 …… 122
鸿雁之什·斯干 …… 125
节南山之什·小弁 …… 129
节南山之什·巧言 …… 135
节南山之什·何人斯 …… 140
节南山之什·巷伯 …… 144

四 绵绵瓜瓞

文王之什·文王 …… 191
文王之什·大明 …… 197
文王之什·绵 …… 203
文王之什·棫朴 …… 208
文王之什·旱麓 …… 210
生民之什·生民 …… 213
生民之什·行苇 …… 220
生民之什·既醉 …… 224
生民之什·凫鹥 …… 228
生民之什·假乐 …… 232
荡之什·荡 …… 237
荡之什·抑 …… 243
荡之什·桑柔 …… 253
荡之什·云汉 …… 263
荡之什·崧高 …… 269

六 于胥乐兮

驷之什·驷 ······ 316
驷之什·有駜 ······ 320
商颂·那 ······ 324
商颂·烈祖 ······ 326
商颂·玄鸟 ······ 328

云谁之思

第一章

CHAPTER ONE

Of whom do you think ahead

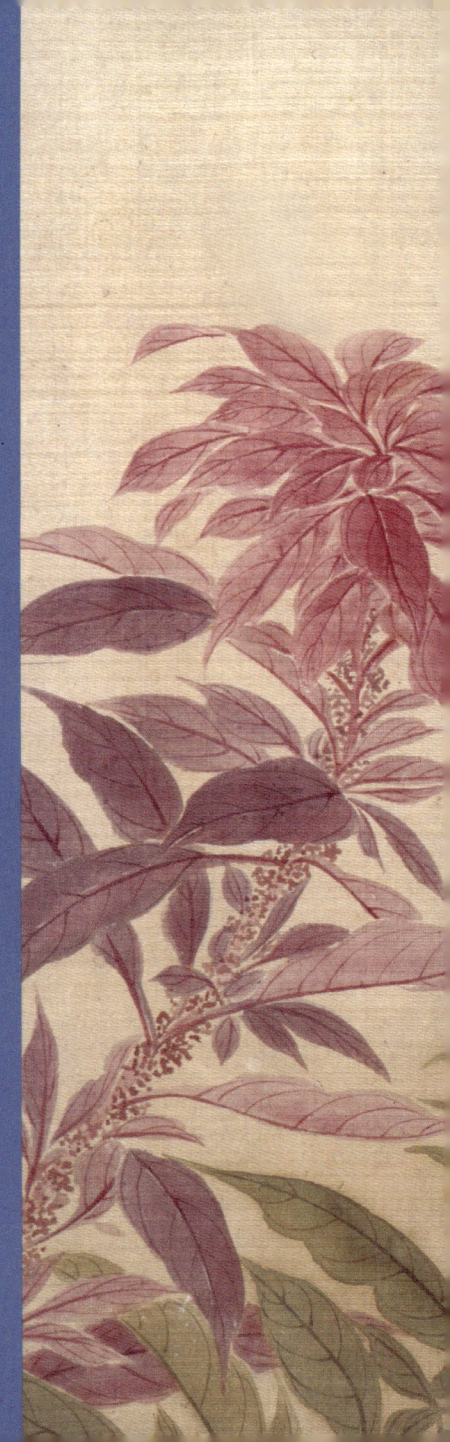

周南·葛覃

葛之覃兮,施于中谷,维叶萋萋。黄鸟于飞,集于灌木,其鸣喈喈。

葛之覃兮,施于中谷,维叶莫莫。是刈是濩,为絺为绤,服之无斁。

言告师氏,言告言归。薄污我私,薄浣我衣。害浣害否,归宁父母。

Home-going of the Bride

The vines outspread and trail
In the midst of the vale.
Their leaves grow lush and sprout;
Yellow birds fly about
And perch on leafy trees.
O how their twitters please!

The vines outspread and trail
In the midst of the vale.
Their leaves grow lush on soil,
So good to cut and boil
And make cloth coarse or fine.
Who wears it likes the vine.

I tell Mother-in-law.
Soon I will homeward go.
I'll wash my undershirt
And rinse my outerskirt.
My dress cleaned, I'll appear
Before my parents dear.

你看那葛藤长长，蔓延于山谷，叶片何其茂盛。

你看那黄雀飞起，又齐齐落于灌木，喈喈鸣叫不已。

你看那葛藤长长，蔓延于山谷，叶片何其茂密。

收割藤蔓拿去煮，做成粗布细布的衣服，舒舒服服穿在身上。

我要去告诉我的保姆，我想归省回娘家。

且去洗我的家常衣裳，再洗华服盛装。

该洗哪些？该放下哪些？反正我要去看我的爹娘。

主人公已为人妇，还保持着活泼心性。在一个好天气里，她想做一些让自己更快乐的事。她看上去在挑选各种衣服，其实挑选的是对幸福场景的想象。想象要见的人，要赶赴的盛宴，而这些泡沫般涌来的场景里，最让她感到幸福的，是她终于能隔着尘埃与路途，看见站在门口的爹娘。

周南·螽斯

螽斯羽,诜诜兮。宜尔子孙,振振兮。
螽斯羽,薨薨兮。宜尔子孙,绳绳兮。
螽斯羽,揖揖兮。宜尔子孙,蛰蛰兮。

Blessed with Children

Insects in flight,
Well you appear.
It is all right
To teem with children dear.

Insects in flight,
How sound your wings!
It is all right
To have children in strings.

Insects in flight,
You feel so warm.
It is all right
To have children in swarm.

螽虫啊你支棱着翅膀，密密麻麻，遮天蔽日。

你子嗣众多，家族兴旺，看得我心里冰冰凉。

螽虫啊你支棱着翅膀，嗡嗡地响。

你子嗣众多，世代绵延，看得我心里很绝望。

螽虫啊你支棱着翅膀，在我的庄稼地里聚会忙。

你子嗣众多，儿孙满堂，把快乐建立在我的痛苦上。

通常认为这首诗旨在祝福子嗣不绝，《诗序》说是赞扬后妃不妒，子孙众多。清代学者马瑞辰认为古文"宜"作"多"，"'宜尔子孙'，犹云多尔子孙"，并没有颂扬之意。

①诜诜：众多。②薨薨：象声词，形容虫飞的声音。③揖揖：聚集。

召南·采蘩

于以采蘩？于沼于沚。于以用之？公侯之事。

于以采蘩？于涧之中。于以用之？公侯之宫。

被之僮僮，夙夜在公。被之祁祁，薄言还归。

The Sacrifice

Gather southernwood white
By the pools here and there.
Employ it in the rite.
In our prince's affair.

Gather southernwood white
In the vale by the stream.
Employ it in the rite
Under the temple's beam.

Wearing black, gloosy hair,
We're busy all the day.
With disheveled hair
At dusk we go away.

你去哪里采白蒿，去水边的小洲，飘着白雾的湖沼。

采来白蒿有何用？放在公侯家的祭桌上。

你去哪里采白蒿？在那湍急的山涧中。

采来白蒿有何用？呈在公侯家的祖庙里。

你鬓间珠翠闪闪，为家中事务从早忙到晚。

你的黑发繁茂如森林，直到深夜你才回到家里。

通常说，这首诗描述公侯夫人亲力亲为于家族祭祀。是辛劳，也是荣誉，就像《红楼梦》里的王熙凤，累并快乐着，亲手操持家族中的仪式，才会感到被全面接纳。

召南·行露

①厌浥行露,岂不夙夜,谓行多露。

谁谓雀无角?何以穿我屋?谁谓女无家?

何以速我狱?②虽速我狱,室家不足!

谁谓鼠无牙?何以穿我墉?谁谓女无家?

何以速我讼?虽速我讼,亦不女从!

I Accuse

The path with dew is wet;
Before dawn of I set;
I fear nor dew nor threat.

Who says in sparrow's head
No beak can pierce the roof?
Who says the man's not wed?
He jails me without proof.
He can't wed me in jail;
I'm jailed to no avail.

Who says in the rat's head
No teeth can pierce the wall?
Who says the man's not wed?
He brings me to judge's hall.
Though brought to judge's hall.
I will not yield at all.

露水打湿幽暗的路，我的脚步如此匆促，有人问我为何疾行于黑夜，我说早晨道上有更多露。

谁说麻雀没有嘴，为啥它能啄穿我的屋？

谁说你家没有妻？为何将我朝监狱里逼。

就算你发誓将我送进监狱，你这逼婚的理由也不成立。

谁说老鼠没有牙，为什么在我家墙上打洞。

谁说你家无妻室，为啥送我上公堂？

就算被你告上公堂，要我从你是休想。

　　中国古代"白毛女"的故事，有妇之夫逼女子嫁给他，否则就要对簿公堂——当然，他是能找到理由的。女子不得不趁夜逃走，路途迢迢，夜露沾衣，她誓死不屈服。她的奔走，悲伤而激愤；抗争者的灵魂，是黑夜里的一道光。

①厌浥：湿。②速：导致。

召南·何彼襛矣①

何彼襛(nóng)矣,唐棣之华?曷不肃雍②?王姬之车。

何彼襛矣,华如桃李?平王之孙,齐侯之子。

其钓维何?维丝伊缗(mín)。齐侯之子,平王之孙。

The Princess' Wedding

Luxuriant in spring
As plum flowers o'er water,
How we revere the string
Of cabs for the king's daughter!

Luxuriant in spring
As the peach flowers red,

The daughter of the king
To a marquis' son is wed.

we use the silken thread
To form a fishing line.
The son of marquis is wed
To the princess divine.

那边何事如此盛大,像棠梨花开得如火如荼?

为何肃穆又雍容?是王姬乘车出行。

那边何事如此盛大,繁华如桃李绽放?

是平王孙女,嫁了齐侯的儿子。

钓鱼的丝线有啥讲究?要用丝绳合成股。

就像豪门结姻缘,齐侯之子,堪配平王孙女。

　　这首诗和《桃夭》都描述了迎娶新嫁娘的场景,但《桃夭》是近处视角,这首诗的作者更像站在远处,遥望这一场热闹。强强联合的大婚,普通人只有啧啧称奇的份儿。诗里看不到具体的人,只有"炙手可热势绝伦"的声势。

①禯:盛。②肃雍:庄严雍和。

邶风·简兮

简兮简兮,方将万舞。日之方中,在前上处。
硕人俣俣,公庭万舞。有力如虎,执辔如组。
左手执龠,右手秉翟。赫如渥赭,公言锡爵。
山有榛,隰有苓。云谁之思?西方美人。彼美人兮,西方之人兮。

A Dancer

With main and might
Dances the ace.
Sun at its height,
He holds his place.

He dances long
With might and main.
Like tiger strong
He holds the rein.

A flute in his left hand,
In his right a plume fine.
Red-faced, he holds command,
Given a cup of wine.

Hazel above,
Sweet grass below.
Who is not sick for love
Of the dancing Beau?
Who is not sick for love
Of the Western Beau?

多么威武，他们就要起舞。
像太阳照在正中央，那个人光芒四射，站在最前方。

身姿修长，身形健壮，他们在宫廷中起舞。
孔武有力，威武如虎，手持缰绳如丝带般挥舞。

左手拿着籥管，右手摇动翎毛。
红脸膛像染了赭色。公侯命人赐他们一杯酒。

高高的山上有榛树，低矮的湿地长苦苓。
你问我到底在想念谁，我说是打西边来的那好看的人。
那个好看的人，他是从西边过来的啊。

万舞是一场集体舞，由文舞和武舞组成。这个领舞的人，身强力壮，左右开弓，有着显著的异族情调，打动了女子的芳心。然而那又怎样呢？他们之间咫尺天涯，他所吸引她的那种陌生感，同时也无情地将她阻隔。

①简兮：说法很多，一说威武之意；也有解释为鼓声；还有选拔之说。朱熹说是"简易不恭"。

邶风·柏舟

泛彼柏舟,在彼中河。髧彼两髦,实维我仪。之死矢靡它。母也天只!不谅人只!

泛彼柏舟,在彼河侧。髧彼两髦,实维我特。之死矢靡慝。母也天只!不谅人只!

A Cypress Boat

A cypress boat
Midstream afloat.
Two tufts of hair o'er his forehead,
He is my mate to whom I'll wed.
I swear I won't change my mind till I'm dead.
Heaven and mother,
Why don't you understand another?

A cypress boat
By riverside afloat.
Two tufts of hair o'er his forehead,
He is my only mate to whom I'll wed.
I swear I won't change my mind though dead.
Heaven and mother,
Why don't you understand another?

柏舟摇摇晃晃，漂在大河中央。

眼前这个少年，长发在耳边飞扬，是我心仪的模样。

我发誓，死都不会把别人放在心上。

母亲啊，你冷酷如上天，总也不能将我体谅。

柏舟摇摇晃晃，漂在河道一旁。

眼前这个少年，长发在耳边飞扬，是我心仪的模样。

我发誓，死也不会改变心中主张。

母亲啊，你冷酷如上天，总也不能将我体谅。

一个私奔的少女，和心上人奔赴未知，心如涟漪，彷徨不定。但她转头看见所爱，知道自己不可能再有别的选择，反过来抱怨母亲的心如铁石。

是啊，那个当娘的人，你看到女儿的爱情在闪耀，就不曾想到自己的少女时代，心里有那么一点点松动吗？

鄘风·桑中

爰采唐矣？沬之乡矣。云谁之思？美孟姜矣。期我乎桑中，要我乎上宫，送我乎淇之上矣。

爰采麦矣？沬之北矣。云谁之思？美孟弋矣。期我乎桑中，要我乎上宫，送我乎淇之上矣。

爰采葑矣？沬之东矣。云谁之思？美孟庸矣。期我乎桑中，要我乎上宫，送我乎淇之上矣。

Trysts

"Where gather golden thread?" "In the fields over there."
"Of whom do you think ahead?" "Jiang's eldest daughter fair.
She did wait for me 'neath mulberry, In upper bower tryst with me
And see me of on River Qi."

"Where gather golden wheat?" "In northern fields o'er there."
"Whom do you long to meet?" "Yi's eldest daughter fair.
She did wait for me 'neath mulberry, In upper bower tryst with me
And see me of on River Qi."

"Where gather mustard plant?" "In eastern fields o'er there."
"Who does your heart enchant?" "Yong's eldest daughter fair.
She did wait for me 'neath mulberry, In upper bower tryst with me
And see me of on River Qi."

要采女萝去哪里？沬邑的郊外啊。
　　你问我心中念着谁，美丽的孟姜啊。
　　她期待我于桑园，邀请我去楼上，又把我送到淇水边啊。

　　要采麦穗去哪里？沬邑的北边啊。
　　你问我心里念着谁，美丽的孟弋啊。
　　她期待我于桑园，邀请我去楼上，又把我送到淇水边啊。

　　要采芜菁去哪里？沬邑的东边啊。
　　你问我心里念着谁，美丽的孟庸啊。
　　她期待我于桑园，邀请我去楼上，又把我送到淇水边啊。

　　孟姜、孟弋和孟庸，都是美女的代称。有人说，这首诗展现了一个男人的意淫，他想象自己和三个美女约会。中国现代历史学家顾颉刚论证实为一人。

　　男子也许并没有一个真实的恋人，只是在心中有个若有若无的影像。像很多人一样，他渴望的不是爱人，而是爱情存在的场景。

鄘风·蝃蝀

蝃(dì)蝀(dōng)在东,莫之敢指。
女子有行,远父母兄弟。

朝跻(jī)于西,崇朝其雨。
女子有行,远兄弟父母。

乃如之人也,怀昏姻也。
大无信也,不知命也!

Elopement

A rainbow rose high in the east;
None dared to point to it at least.
I went to wed like others
And left my parents and my brothers.

The morning clouds rose in the west;
The day with rain would then be blest.
I went to wed another
When I left my father and mother.

Did I know I'd be raped by such a man
Who would do whatever he can!
He is a faithless mate.
Is it my fault or fate?

彩虹悬挂在东方,谁敢以手相指?

女子要嫁人,远离父母和兄弟。

彩虹悬挂在西方,雨落了一早晨。

女子要嫁人,远离兄弟和父母。

像这样一个人啊,不按正道来婚配。

完全不管信义名誉,父母教导也不理。

在古代,彩虹是不祥之兆,这个女子奔赴的,应该是一桩不被父母和兄弟认可的婚姻。在古代,婚姻更多意味着职责。激情则是危险的,就像这无处不在的彩虹。一方面暗喻着私奔的放荡,另一方面也警示着这孤注一掷的奔赴,凶险多多。

鄘风·相鼠

相鼠有皮,人而无仪!人而无仪,不死何为?

相鼠有齿,人而无止!人而无止,不死何俟?

相鼠有体,人而无礼!人而无礼,胡不遄死?

The Rat

The rat has skin, you see?
Man must have decency.
If he lacks decency,
Worse than death it would be.

The rat has teeth, you see?
Man must have dignity.
If he lacks dignity,
For what but death waits he?

The rat has limbs, you see?
Man must have propriety.
Without propriety,
It's better dead to be.

你看老鼠尚且有皮,做人怎能不讲礼仪。

人要是不讲礼仪,不去死还想干什么?

你看老鼠尚且有齿,做人怎能不知耻?

做人要是不知耻,不死还想等啥呢?

你看老鼠尚且有身体,做人怎能不讲礼义?

做人要是不讲礼义,还不赶紧去死?

体面是最后的约束,完全不讲体面的人,你是拿他没办法的。作者已经出奇愤怒,失去理性,只能骂对方为什么不去死。《白虎通·谏诤篇》解释为:"妻得谏夫者,夫妇一体,荣辱共之",但这明显是骂不是谏,而且真心不想"共之"了。

鄘风·干旄

孑孑干旄,在浚之郊。素丝纰之,良马四之。
彼姝者子,何以畀之?

孑孑干旟,在浚之都。素丝组之,良马五之。
彼姝者子,何以予之?

孑孑干旌,在浚之城。素丝祝之,良马六之。
彼姝者子,何以告之?

Betrothal Gifts

The flags with ox-tail tied
Flutter in countryside.
Adorned with silk bands white,
Four steeds trot left and right.
What won't I give and share
With such a maiden faire?

The falcon-banners fly
In the outskirts nearby.
Adorned with ribbons white,
Five steeds trot left and right.
What won't I give and send
To such a good fair friend?

The feathered streamers go down
All the way to the town.
Bearing rolls of silk white,
Six steeds trot left and right.
What and how should I say.
To her as fair as May?

特地挂出牦牛尾装饰的旗,晃荡在浚邑郊外。
你的旗子用白丝线缝就,好马四匹在你左右。
可是那个美好的人,你拿什么来给她?

特地挂出绣着鹰隼的旗,晃荡在浚邑的城镇。
你的旗子用白丝线缝就,好马五匹在你左右。
可是那个美好的人,你拿什么送给她?

特地挂出野鸡毛装饰的旗,晃荡在浚邑城中。
你的旗子用白丝线缝就,好马六匹在你左右。
可是那个美好的人,你怎样把心事说给她听?

《毛诗序》说这首诗是"美好善者",也就是夸奖喜欢善行的人。然而这番阵势,似与善行无关,更像是富家子弟不知道如何追求心中的白月光,只能全副披挂,不断加码,试图吸引对方。可惜"彼姝者子"无动于衷,"何以畀之""何以予之""何以告之"的自问背后,是爱而不得的抓耳挠腮。

卫风·芄兰

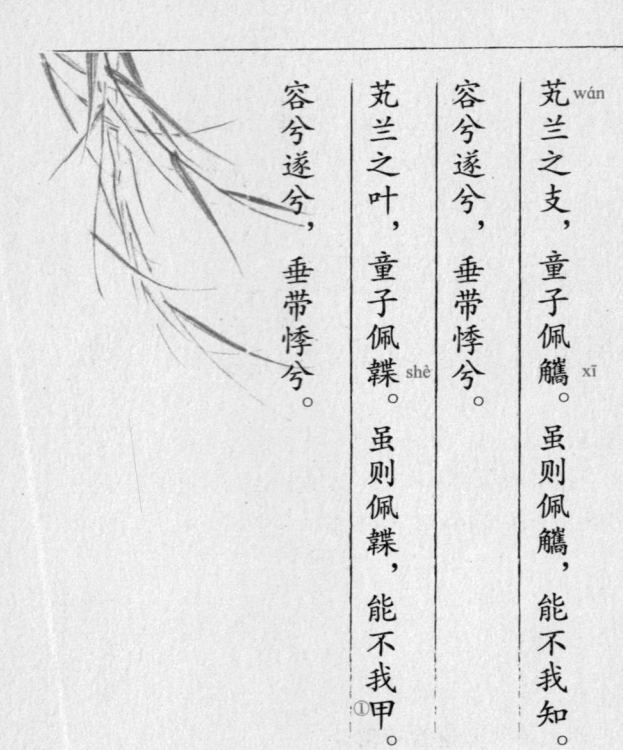

芄兰之支,童子佩觿。虽则佩觿,能不我知。
容兮遂兮,垂带悸兮。

芄兰之叶,童子佩韘。虽则佩韘,能不我甲。
容兮遂兮,垂带悸兮。

A Widow in Love

The creeper's pods hang like
The young man's girdle spike.
An adult's spike he wears;
For us he no longer cares.
He puts on airs and swings
To and fro tassel-strings.

The creeper's leaves also swing;
The youth wears archer's ring.
An archer's ring he wears;
For us he no longer cares.
He puts on airs and swings
To and fro tassel-strings.

芄兰枝条像什么?像少年身上能解开衣带的角锥。

虽然你佩戴了角锥,却不能解我情意。

你的仪容啊,你的姿态啊,你垂下的丝带轻轻摆动啊。

芄兰的叶子像什么?像少年手上戴的扳指啊。

你戴了扳指很神气,不与我亲狎也白搭。

你的仪容啊,你的姿态啊,你垂下的丝带轻轻摆动啊。

多情女子对于直男的抱怨:他带了能解开衣带的角锥却不知道如何使用;他的心思更多地放在拉弓射箭上,随手带着扳指。他自己觉得玉树临风、潇洒不可一世,但在姑娘心中,可能是个"后来就没有后来了"的故事。

①甲:狎。

卫风·伯兮

伯兮朅兮,邦之桀兮。伯也执殳,为王前驱。

自伯之东,首如飞蓬。岂无膏沐,谁适为容?

其雨其雨,杲杲出日。愿言思伯,甘心首疾。

焉得谖草,言树之背。愿言思伯,使我心痗。

My Lord

My lord is brave and bright,
A hero in our land,
A vanguard in King's fight,
With a lance in his hand.

Since my lord eastward went,
Like thistle looks my hair.
Have I no anointment?
For whom should I look fair?

Let it rain, let it rain!
The sun shines bright instead.
I miss my lord in vain,
Heedless of aching head.

Where's the Herb to Forget?
To plant it north I'd start.
Missing my lord, I fret:
It makes me sick at heart.

我的夫君何其英武，是这城邦里的俊杰。

我的夫君手执殳杖，冲锋在先，为君王开路。

夫君自从你去了东方，我头发乱如野草飞蓬。

难道没有胭脂香膏？但是你不在，我无法为悦己者容。

有时候天会下雨，有时候忽然见日出。

不管是晴天还是雨天，夫君，我只想念你，纵然这思念令我头痛难忍，我也甘之如饴。

到哪里寻找那忘忧草，将它种在北堂。

夫君，我是如此的想念你，这思念像一场心疾，等你来医。

爱情会带来强烈的失重感。一方面，她为心上人的英武感到骄傲，另一方面，这英武正是他离开她的缘由。日常变得紊乱，原本修饰仪表是人的本能，但他不在，这世界便空无一人。下雨还是日出对她来说都一样，世间差别只在于，他在，或他不在。

王风·黍离

彼黍离离,彼稷之苗。行迈靡靡,中心摇摇。
知我者,谓我心忧;不知我者,谓我何求。
悠悠苍天,此何人哉?

彼黍离离,彼稷之穗。行迈靡靡,中心如醉。
知我者,谓我心忧;不知我者,谓我何求。
悠悠苍天,此何人哉?

彼黍离离,彼稷之实。行迈靡靡,中心如噎。
知我者,谓我心忧;不知我者,谓我何求。
悠悠苍天,此何人哉?

The Ruined Capital

The millet drops its head;
The sorghum is in sprout.
Slowly I trudge and tread;
My heart is tossed about.
Those who know me will say
My heart is sad and bleak;
Those who don't know me may
Ask me for what I seek.
O boundless azure sky,
Who's ruined the land and why?

The millet drops its head;
The sorghum in the ear.
Slowly I trudge and tread;
My heart seems drunk and drear
Those who know me will say
My heart is sad and bleak;
Those who don't know me may
Ask me for what I seek.
O boundless azure sky,
Who's ruined the land and why?

The millet drops its head;
The sorghum is in grain.
Slowly I trudge and tread;
My heart seems choked with pain.
Those who know me will say
My heart is sad and bleak;
Those who don't know me may
Ask me for what I seek.
O boundless azure sky,
Who's ruined the land and why?

黍子成行，高粱抽条。
慢慢走在路上，心事飘摇。
懂我的人，知道我心忧。
不懂我的人，问我还有何求。
悠悠苍天，这是怎样的人生？

黍子成行，高粱结穗。
慢慢走在路上，心中如醉。
懂我的人，知道我心忧。
不懂我的人，问我还有何求。
悠悠苍天，这是怎样的人生？

黍子成行，高粱正在结实。
慢慢走在路上，无法呼吸。
懂我的人，知道我心忧。
不懂我的人，问我还有何求。
悠悠苍天，这是怎样的人生？

不被懂得，是人的宿命。《红楼梦》里贾探春说："外头看着我们不知千金万金小姐，何等快乐，殊不知我们这里说不出来的烦难，更利害。"

除了现实的煎熬，还有诗与远方的诱惑，就像《立春》里的王彩玲，内心始终处于动荡之中。但她的不甘都被视为瞎折腾，无人理解她为什么不甘心岁月静好。

王风·扬之水

扬之水,不流束薪。彼其之子,不与我戍申。怀哉怀哉,曷月予还归哉?

扬之水,不流束楚。彼其之子,不与我戍甫。怀哉怀哉,曷月予还归哉?

扬之水,不流束蒲。彼其之子,不与我戍许。怀哉怀哉,曷月予还归哉?

In Garrison

Slowly the water flows;
Firewood can't be carried away.
You're afraid of your foes;
Why don't you in garrison stay?
How much for home I yearn!
O when may I return?

Slowly the water flows;
No thorn can be carried away.
You're afraid of your foes;
Why don't you in army camps stay?
How much for home I yearn!
O when may I return?

Slowly the water flows;
Rushes can't be carried away.
You're afraid of your foes;
Why don't you in army tents stay?
How much for home I yearn?
O when may I return?

水流激荡，却带不走一捆干柴。
我想念的那个人，不能陪我戍守申地。
我相思成灾，到底哪年哪月才能回归故里？

水流激荡，却带不走一捆荆条。
我想念的那个人，不能陪我戍守甫地。
我相思成灾，到底哪年哪月才能回归故里？

水流激荡，却带不走一捆旱柳。
我想念的那个人，不能陪我戍守许地。
我相思成灾，到底哪年哪月才能回归故里？

"扬"意为激扬，他的感情那么激荡，却无法将所爱者一起带走，对方留在原地，他却要在申、甫、许等地迁徙。不管他走到哪里，和她的距离都在那里。他拼命地想念，她的形象模糊如家乡，而归期难测，所有的努力终究化作徒劳。

王风·丘中有麻

丘中有麻,彼留子嗟。彼留子嗟,将其来施施。

丘中有麦,彼留子国。彼留子国,将其来食。

丘中有李,彼留之子。彼留之子,贻我佩玖。

To Her Lover

Hemp on the mound I see.
Who's there detaining thee?
Who's there detaining thee?
From coming jauntily to me?

Wheat on the mound I'm thinking of.
Who detains thee above?
Who detains thee above
From coming with me to make love?

On the mound stands plum tree.
Who's there detaining thee?
Who's there detaining thee
From giving girdle gems to me?

> 山坡中间有苎麻啊,那个留子嗟。那个留子嗟啊,我等待你施施然而来。
>
> 山坡中间有麦苗啊,那个留子国。那个留子国啊,我有美味待你品尝。
>
> 山坡中间有李子啊,那个留之子。那个留之子啊,你送我的美玉我戴在身上。

女子大胆提出约会,所谓"有麻""有麦""有李",归根结底是暗示"有我"。"子嗟""子国"和"之子",可能和"孟姜""孟弋"和"孟庸"代指美女一样,指的是同一个美男子。

"留",让南宋时期理学家朱熹困惑,认为这首诗讲的女子与男子约会,担心他被别人"留"住了,表达的是患得患失之感。清代学者王先谦所著《诗三家义集疏》则称"留"不过是男子的姓。

郑风·缁衣

缁衣之宜兮,敝予又改为兮。
适子之馆兮,还予授子之粲兮①。
缁衣之好兮,敝予又改造兮。
适子之馆兮,还予授子之粲兮。
缁衣之席兮,敝予又改作兮。
适子之馆兮,还予授子之粲兮。

A Good Wife

The black-dyed robe befits you well;
When it's worn out, I'll make another new.
You go to work in your hotel;
Come back, I'll make a meal for you.

The black-dyed robe becomes you well;
When it's worn out, I'll get another new.
You go to work in your hotel;
Come back, I'll make a meal for you.

The black-dyed robe does suit you well;
When it's worn out, you'll have another new.
You go to work in your hotel;
Come back, I'll make a meal for you.

这件黑衣多合身,破了,我帮你重新做啊。

你穿了它去官衙,回来,我给你端上美味的饭菜。

这件黑衣多么好,破了,我帮你再去改造啊。

你穿了它去官衙,回来,我给你端上美味的饭菜。

这件黑衣宽且大,破了,我帮你再去改做啊。

你穿了它去官衙,回来,我给你端上美味的饭菜。

妻子端详着丈夫的官服,看到了当下的幸福,和未来的希望,喜不自胜。中国现代社会学家费孝通在《乡土中国》里说,中国的家是一个事业组织。这个家庭,就在齐心协力谋发展,丈夫在外面工作,妻子在家操持,以达到自洽。

①粲:通"餐"。

郑风·萚兮

萚兮萚兮(tuò),风其吹女。叔兮伯兮,倡予和女。

萚兮萚兮,风其漂女。叔兮伯兮,倡予要女。

Sing Together

Leaves sear, leaves sear,
The wind blows you away.
Sing, cousins dear,
And I'll join in your lay.

Leaves sear, leaves sear,
The wind wafts you away.
Sing, cousins dear,
And I'll complete your lay.

树叶落了,树叶落了,大风将你吹起来了。
弟弟啊,哥哥啊,我来领唱你来和啊。

树叶落了,树叶落了,大风将你吹起来了。
弟弟啊,哥哥啊,我来领唱你来和啊。

像是一首秋风起时随风而舞的歌谣,唱出季节转化时的快乐。风吹落叶引发的不一定是伤感,还有在风中像树叶一样起舞的兴致。

郑风·丰

子之丰兮,俟我乎巷兮,
悔予不送兮。

子之昌兮,俟我乎堂兮,
悔予不将兮。

衣锦褧衣,裳锦褧裳。
叔兮伯兮,驾予与行。

裳锦褧裳,衣锦褧衣。
叔兮伯兮,驾予与归。

Lost Opportunity

You looked plump and plain
And waited for me in the lane.
Why did I not go with you? I complain.

You looked strong and tall
And waited for me in the hall.
I regret I did not return your call.

Over my broidered skirt
I put on simple shirt.
O Sir, to you I say:
Come in your cab and let us drive away!

I put on simple shirt
Over my broidered skirt.
O Sir, I say anew:
Come in your cab and take me home with you!

他的背影多么高大，等我在巷子里，真后悔没有送你啊。

他的背影多么健壮，等我在堂屋里，真后悔没有跟你走啊。

且等有一天，我上穿锦绣外衣，下着锦绣长裙。
我的弟弟与哥哥，赶着马车送我去和你在一起。

我下着锦绣长裙，上穿锦绣外衣。
我的弟弟与哥哥，赶着马车送我和你一起回家去。

男子前来相约，女子心情复杂，纵然郎情妾意，私下约会也多少有些冒险。女子像《氓》里的女主人公那样拒绝了男子，当他离开时，她后悔起来，内心的冲动，与世间禁忌发生冲突。

与其悔之晚矣，不如畅想未来。通过父母之命媒妁之言的准许后，她精心打扮后去跟他见面。快乐虽然来得晚一点，但延时满足让人心里更踏实一点。

郑风·溱洧

溱与洧,方涣涣兮。士与女,方秉蕳兮。女曰观乎?士曰既且,且往观乎!洧之外,洵訏且乐。维士与女,伊其相谑,赠之以勺药。

溱与洧,浏其清矣。士与女,殷其盈矣。女曰观乎?士曰既且,且往观乎!洧之外,洵訏且乐。维士与女,伊其将谑,赠之以勺药。

Riverside Rendezvous

The Rivers Zhen and Wei
Overflow on their way.
The lovely lad and lass
Hold in hand fragrant grass.
"Let's look around, "says she;
"I've already, "says he.
"Let us go there again!
Beyond the River Wei
The ground is large and people gay."
Playing together then,
They have a happy hour;
Each gives the other peony flower.

The Rivers Zhen and Wei
Flow crystal-clear;
Lad and lass squeeze their way
Through the crowd full of cheer.
"Let's look around, "says she;
"I've already, "says he.
"Let us go there again!
Beyond the River Wei
The ground is large and people gay."
Playing together then,
They have a happy hour;
Each gives the other peony flower.

溱水与洧水,刚刚满涨。
少年与姑娘,兰草拿在手上。
姑娘说,去那边看看?
少年说,虽已看过,再去看一回又何妨!
洧水边,实在开阔又热闹。
少年与姑娘,互相开着玩笑,赠对方以芍药。

溱水与洧水,看上去多么清澈。
姑娘与少年,摩肩接踵。
姑娘说,去那边看看?
少年说,虽已看过,再去看一回又何妨。
洧水边,实在开阔又热闹。
少年与姑娘,互相开着玩笑,赠对方以芍药。

  溱水与洧水之畔,春光大好的上巳节,
少年遇见了姑娘。虽然有些热闹他已经看过,
但跟她一起看的热闹,就是另外一场热闹。

清扬婉兮

第二章

CHAPTER TWO

With keenest sight

齐风·还

子之还兮,遭我乎峱(náo)之间兮。并驱从两肩兮,
揖我谓我儇(xuān)兮。

子之茂兮,遭我乎峱之道兮。并驱从两牡兮,
揖我谓我好兮。

子之昌兮,遭我乎峱之阳兮。并驱从两狼兮,
揖我谓我臧兮。

Two Hunters

How agile you appear!
Amid the hills we meet.
Pursuing two boars, compeer,
You bow and say I'm fleet.

How skilful you appear!
We meet halfway uphill.
Driving after two males, compeer,
You bow and praise my skill.

How artful you appear!
South of the hill we meet.
Pursuing two wolves, compeer,
You bow and say my art's complete.

你轻捷矫健，和我相遇在猺山间。

我们一同追赶两只野兽，你拱手赞扬我的灵活。

你技艺超群，和我相遇在猺山道上。

我们一同追赶两只公兽，你拱手赞扬我手段高。

你健壮有力，和我相遇在猺山之南。

我们一同追赶两匹狼，你拱手赞扬我本事好。

  两个猎人在猺山邂逅，虽素昧平生，但齐心协力。两人都是高手，这场围猎因此有了游戏的效果，像两个配合默契的足球运动员，为对方每一个精彩表现鼓掌。生活中，并不是只有爱情才会有过电的感觉，工作中的惺惺相惜，同样能让人激情四射，实现共赢。

齐风·著

俟我于著乎而,充耳以素乎而,尚之以琼华乎而。
俟我于庭乎而,充耳以青乎而,尚之以琼莹乎而。
俟我于堂乎而,充耳以黄乎而,尚之以琼英乎而。

The Bridegroom

He waits for me between the door and screen,
His crown adorned with ribbons green
Ended with gems of beautiful sheen.

He waits for me in the court with delight,
His crown adorned with ribbons white
Ended with gems and rubies bright.

He waits for me in inner hall,
His crown adorned with yellow ribbons all
Ended with gems like golden ball.

他等候我，在大门和屏风之间。

白色丝线系瑱玉，挂在冠之两边，还有赤玉雕花，镶嵌在帽檐。

他等候我，在我家的内院。

青色丝线系瑱玉，挂在冠之两边，还有赤玉雕花，镶嵌在帽檐。

他等候我，在我家的厅堂。

黄色丝线系瑱玉，挂在冠之两边。还有赤玉雕花，镶嵌在帽檐。

　　这首诗写的是新娘等待新郎迎娶的场景，新郎身着盛装，步步行来。所谓充耳，是古人用丝线系上名为"瑱"的玉石，挂在帽子两边。新郎充耳上的丝线忽而白，忽而青，忽而黄，这不重要，就像诗里把美女忽而唤作孟姜，忽而唤作孟弋一样，我们只要知道，它是新娘眼中最美的颜色。

齐风·东方之日

东方之日兮,彼姝者子,在我室兮。
在我室兮,履我即兮。
东方之月兮,彼姝者子,在我闼兮。
在我闼兮,履我发兮。①

Nocturnal Tryst

The eastern sun is red;
The maiden like a bloom
Follows me to my room.
The maiden in my room.
Follows me to the bed.

The eastern moon is bright;
The maiden I adore
Follows me out of door.
The maiden out of door
Leaves me and goes out of sight.

东边的太阳啊,你看那美丽的女子,在我的屋子里啊。

在我的屋子里,踩着我的脚印啊。

东方的月亮啊,你看那美丽的女子,在我的屋子里啊。

在我的屋子里,踩着我的行迹啊。

像《西厢记》里,张生看见崔莺莺突然出现在房中,有一种巨大的不真实感,以至于要呼喊太阳和月亮作证。即便如此,他还是无法觉得她这个人是真的,看见她的脚步踩着自己走过的地方,坐在自己坐过的苇席上,终于觉得幻想叠印上了现实。

①发:行去。朱熹译为"言蹑我而行去也"。

齐风·甫田

无田甫田,维莠骄骄。无思远人,劳心忉忉。
无田甫田,维莠桀桀。无思远人,劳心怛怛。
婉兮娈兮。总角丱(guàn)兮。未几见兮,突而弁兮!

Missing Her Son

Don't till too large a ground,
Or weed will spread around.
Don't miss one far away,
Or you'll grieve night and day.

Don't till too large a ground,
Or weed overgrows around.
Don't miss the far-of one,
Or your grief won't be done.

My son was young and fair
With his two tufts of hair.
Not seen for a short time,
He's grown up to his prime.

若是力量小，别去种大田，野草恣意长，让你空叹息。

若是命中无缘，别惦记已经离开的人，枉自耗费心神，伸手也无法触及。

若是力量小，别去种大田，野草恣意长，让你空叹息。

若是命中无缘，别惦记已经离开的人，枉自耗费心神，他与你无关。

难忘年少时候，我们扎着小辫，之后睽隔多年，他突然戴上成人冠冕。

爱上一个不可能的人，大概就像独自种一大片田地，貌似有无限可能，真相却可能是有心无力。播种下爱恋，收获的只是荒芜。她知道这一切都是徒劳，但还是忍不住回溯到久别重逢那一刻——过去瞬间复苏，已经长大的他，让她心动，但不再熟悉。

齐风·猗嗟

猗嗟昌兮,颀而长兮。抑若扬兮,美目扬兮。
巧趋跄兮,射则臧兮。
猗嗟名兮,美目清兮。仪既成兮,终日射侯,
不出正兮,展我甥兮。
猗嗟娈兮,清扬婉兮。舞则选兮,射则贯兮。
四矢反兮,以御乱兮。

The Archer Duke

Fairest of all,
He's grand and tall,
His forehead high
With sparkling eye;
He's fleet of foot
And skilled to shoot.

His fame is high
With crystal eye;
In brave array
He shoots all day;
Each shot a hit,
No son's so fit.

He's fair and bright
With keenest sight;
He dances well;
Each shot will tell;
Four shots right go;
He'll quell the foe.

哎呀，这个美少年，身材颀长。

他额头宽广，漂亮眼睛神采飞扬。

进退节奏都优美，射箭的技艺世无双。

哎呀，这少年盛世美颜，漂亮眼睛清澈如水。

成年礼既然已经完成，不妨终日射箭。

每一支箭都不出红圈，真是我的好外甥。

哎呀，这少年真是美好，一双美目神采飞扬。

他舞姿曼妙，又百步穿杨。

四支箭都射中靶心，乱世他也可以抵挡。

    这少年技艺超群长相又好，尤其是一双自信而坚定的眼睛，清澈而又神采飞扬，让人看了忍不住赞叹连连。作为少年的舅舅，更有一种"芝兰玉树生于庭阶"的骄傲，寄予无限希望。

① 昌：美。

魏风·葛屦

纠纠葛屦,可以履霜。掺掺女手,
可以缝裳?要之襋之,好人服之。
好人提提,宛然左辟,佩其象揥。
维是褊心,是以为刺。

A Well-Drest Lady and Her Maid

In summer shoes with silken lace,
A maid walks on frost at quick pace.
By slender fingers of the maid
Her mistress' beautiful attire is made.
The waistband and the collar fair
Are ready now for her mistress to wear.

The lady moves with pride;
She turns her head aside
With ivory pins in her hair.
Against her narrow mind
I'll use satire unkind.

葛麻缠做新鞋，可以踩冰霜。

这一双纤巧小手，可以缝衣裳。

缝了腰身缝领口，华裳制成给贵妇人穿。

贵人脸上有傲气，扭转腰肢向左避，头上戴着象牙簪。

这种心地狭窄之人，我偏要来刺刺她。

女子做衣服鞋履时，相当自信。她在制作中感受到许多乐趣，对于衣服的去向，也充满美好想象。

然而现实很讽刺，所谓"好人"并不是真正的好人，阶层感很强，对缝衣女看不上眼，让她心凉。张爱玲说："在没有人与人交接的场合，我充满了生命的欢悦。"女子若有知，当视为知己。

①掺掺：纤纤。②好人：贵妇人。③揥：簪子，可搔头。④褊心：心胸狭窄。

* 55

魏风·十亩之间

十亩之间兮,桑者闲闲兮,行与子还兮。
十亩之外兮,桑者泄泄兮,行与子逝兮。

Gathering Mulberry

Among ten acres of mulberry
All the planters are free.
Why not come back with me?

Beyond ten acres of mulberry
All the lasses are free.
O come away with me!

十亩桑园之内啊，采桑的人优哉游哉，将要和你一起归来啊。

十亩桑园之外啊，采桑的人乐呵呵啊，将要和你一起离开啊。

守着十亩桑田，是一种比较好的状态。衣食无忧，安然度日，既不好高骛远，也不妄自菲薄，劳动与休息各得其所。

唐风·扬之水

扬之水,白石凿凿。素衣朱襮,从子于沃。
既见君子,云何不乐?

扬之水,白石皓皓。素衣朱绣,从子于鹄。
既见君子,云何其忧?

扬之水,白石粼粼。我闻有命,不敢以告人。

Our Prince

The clear stream flows ahead
And the white rocks out stand.
In our plain dress with collars red,
We follow you to eastern land.
Shall we not rejoice since
We have seen our dear prince?

The clear stream flows ahead
And naked rocks out stand.
In plain dress with sleeves broidered red,
We follow you to northern land.
How can we feel sad since
We have seen our dear prince?

The clear stream flows along the border;
Wave-beaten rocks stand out.
We've heard the secret order,
But nothing should be talked about.

水流激荡，白石清晰。
你素衣朱领，我随你走在沃城。
终于与你见面，还有什么不能释怀。

水流激荡，白石皎洁。
你素衣朱袖，我随你走在鹄城。
终于与你见面，还有什么让我忧伤？

水流激荡，白石粼粼有光。
我听到我的命运已经被注定，不敢告诉别人。

"既见君子，云何不乐？"这种自问的前提是很不快乐。走在他身边，她心中依然藏着忧伤，只是知道忧伤无用，不如拼着快乐一把。尽管流水激荡，依然能看清水底的石子，命运潜伏在那里，拼却一醉，最终还是以悲伤收尾。

①襮：领子。②绣：通袖。

唐风·采苓

采苓采苓，首阳之巅。人之为言，苟亦无信。
舍旃舍旃，苟亦无然。人之为言，胡得焉？

采苦采苦，首阳之下。人之为言，苟亦无与。
舍旃舍旃，苟亦无然。人之为言，胡得焉？

采葑采葑，首阳之东。人之为言，苟亦无从。
舍旃舍旃，苟亦无然。人之为言，胡得焉？

Rumor

Could the sweet water plant be found
On the top of the mountain high?
The rumor going round,
If not believed can't fly.
Put it aside, put it aside
So that it can't prevail.
The rumor spreading far and wide
Will be of no avail.

Could bitter water plant be found
At the foot of the mountain high?
The rumor going round
Is what we should deny.
Put it aside, put it aside
So that it can't prevail.
The rumor spreading far and wide
Will be of no avail.

Could water plants be found
East of the mountain high?
The rumor going round,
If disregarded, will die.
Put it aside, put it aside
So that it can't prevail.
The rumor spreading far and wide
Will be of no avail.

采甘草啊采甘草,在首阳山之巅。
有些人嘴里没实话,实在把信用放一边。
舍弃他啊舍弃他,实在不能当回事。
做人说话不算数,也不知到底图个啥。

采苦菜啊采苦菜,在首阳山脚下。
有些人嘴里没实话,实在不值得睬他。
舍弃他啊舍弃他,实在不能当回事。
做人说话不算数,也不知到底图个啥。

采芜菁啊采芜菁,在首阳山之东。
有些人嘴里没实话,实在不能跟从他。
舍弃他啊舍弃他,实在不能当回事。
做人说话不算数,也不知到底图个啥。

老实人总不能明白,说谎到底图个啥。但骗子未必这么想,对于他们来说,欺骗意味着不劳而获,最起码也有智商碾压的快乐。

这首诗也许更适用于爱情。恋爱中诚实的人也许会吃亏,但真情投入全身心燃烧,也让人心生快乐。撒谎的人内心冰冷,他们也许没有失去什么,但也没得到什么。

①旃:之。

秦风·小戎

小戎俴(jiàn)收,五楘梁辀(zhōu)。游环胁驱,阴靷(yǐn)鋈(wù)续。文茵畅毂,驾我骐馵(zhù)。言念君子,温其如玉。在其板屋,乱我心曲。

四牡孔阜,六辔在手。骐骝是中,騧(guā)骊是骖。龙盾之合,鋈以觼(jué)軜(nà)。言念君子,温其在邑。方何为期?胡然我念之。

俴驷孔群,厹(qiú)矛鋈錞(duì)。蒙伐有苑,虎韔(chàng)镂膺。交韔二弓,竹闭绲縢。言念君子,载寝载兴。厌厌良人,秩秩德音。

A Lord on Expedition

His chariot finely bound,
Crisscrossed with straps around,
Covered with tiger's skin,
Driven by horses twin;
His steeds controlled with reins
Through slip rings like gilt chains;
I think of my lord dear
Far-of on the frontier;
He's pure as jade and plain.
O my heart throbs with pain.

His four fine steeds there stand;
He holds six reins in hand.
The insides have black mane,
Yellow the outside twain.
Dragon shields on two wings,
Buckled up as with strings.
I think of my lord dear
So good on the frontier.
When will he come to me?
Can I be yearning-free?

How fine his team appears!
How bright his trident spears!
His shield bears a carved face;
In tiger's skin bow-case
With bamboo frames and bound.
With strings, two bows are found.
I think of my dear mate,
Rise early and sleep late.
My dear, dear one,
Can I forget the good you've done?

小战车上浅车厢,五根皮条绕在车辕上。

皮带穿过活动的环,银环闪亮,紧扣引车的皮条。

虎皮坐垫,长毂飞旋,青黑夹杂的马匹四蹄雪白。

我思念我那意中人,他戎装在身,却又温柔如玉。

在他驻扎的军营前偶遇,已乱我心曲。

四匹公马何其强壮,六根缰绳拉在手上。

青黑与白蹄的马儿在中间,黑黄两色在两边。

画着龙的盾牌合起来,有舌的环固定住骖马,让它们不要乱动弹。

我思念我的意中人,他被派往遥远的边城。

不知道哪天是归期,叫我如何不想他?

四匹马披着薄金甲,长矛上装着金属套。

巨大的盾牌刻着杂羽纹,虎皮弓囊金光璀璨。

两张弓交错在弓囊,竹棨保护绳索缠。

想起我的意中人,我一会儿睡下一会儿起。

他那样安静温柔的人,早已有进退得当的名声。

这首诗里有一种美妙的反差。诗中这位"君子"应当是个军人，生活在满是戎车弓箭、躁动激昂、富有冲突的时代。然而，他本人却是"温其如玉"，"秩秩德音"。有点像后来三国时期的周瑜，集刚健温柔于一身，难怪会"在其板屋，乱我心曲"。

秦风·渭阳

我送舅氏,日至渭阳。何以赠之?路车乘黄。
我送舅氏,悠悠我思。何以赠之?琼瑰玉佩。

Farewell to Duke Wen of Jin

I see my uncle dear
Of north of River Wei.
What's the gift for one I revere?
Golden cab on the way.

I see my uncle dear
Of and think of my mother.
What's the gift for one she and I revere?
Jewels and gems for her brother.

我为舅舅送行,送到渭水北。

我拿什么送给您?黄马驾驶的大车。

我为舅舅送行,一路心绪悠悠。

我拿什么送给您?美玉做的玉佩。

  传说此诗是秦康公为舅舅重耳写的别离之诗。此诗虽短,却大有意味。

  晋文公重耳被迫在外流亡十九年,他姐姐秦姬生前希望弟弟能够回国有所作为,至死未能如愿。如今,秦康公看着舅舅回去,既有母愿得偿的欣慰,又有和舅舅别离的伤感,还有母亲无法看到这一幕的遗憾,更有政治上的各种考量,内心十分复杂。

秦风·权舆

於我乎，夏屋渠渠，今也每食无余。于嗟乎，
不承权舆！

於我乎，每食四簋，今也每食不饱。于嗟乎，
不承权舆！

Not As Before

Ah me! Where is my house of yore?
Now I've not a great deal
To eat at every meal.
Alas! I can't live as before.

Ah me! Where are my dishes four?
Now hungry I feel at every meal.
Alas! I can't eat as before.

唉，我啊，曾经大碗喝酒大块吃肉，如今吃了这顿愁下顿。

让我怎么不叹息，我没能让当年的盛景延续。

唉，我啊，曾经一顿四个菜，如今顿顿吃不饱。

让我怎么不叹息，我没能让当年的盛景延续。

有点像《红楼梦》的开头，作者同样是在自怨自艾，当年饫甘餍肥，如今瓦灶绳床，忍不住有岁月沧桑之叹。然而，无常才是常态，四季轮转，兴衰更替，坦然接受这一切而不是长吁短叹，才是明智做法。

①夏屋：大食器。也有解释为大屋，但后面说"食无余"，还做食器解。

陈风·墓门

墓门有棘,斧以斯之。
夫也不良,国人知之。
知而不已,谁昔然矣。
墓门有梅,有鸮萃止。
夫也不良,歌以讯之。
讯予不顾,颠倒思予。

The Evil-Doing Usurper

The thorn at burial gate
should soon be cut away;
The usurper of the State
should be exposed to the day;
If he's exposed too late,
He'll still do what he may.

At burial gate there's jujube tree,
On which owls perch all the day long;
The usurper from evil is not free.
Let's warn him by a song!
But he won't listen to our plea,
For he takes right for wrong.

墓门有棵荆棘树，拿起斧子砍掉它。
那人为人太差劲，国人早就看透他。
看透也不能阻止他，向来就是这德性。

墓门有棵梅花树，站着一群猫头鹰。
那个人为人太差劲，我只能编个歌儿警告他。
我的警告他不听，等到灾难降临才会想起我。

身居高位者品行低劣，即便大家都心知肚明，也不能拿他怎么样。只能以歌谣的形式谇骂他。但对于一个无法无天的人，这种警告就是耳旁风。诗人只能想象：这人遇到灾祸，也许会想起自己。

桧风·羔裘

羔裘逍遥,狐裘以朝。
岂不尔思?劳心忉忉。

羔裘翱翔,狐裘在堂。
岂不尔思?我心忧伤。

羔裘如膏,日出有曜。
岂不尔思?中心是悼。

The Last Lord of Kuai

You seek amusement in official dress;
You hold your court in sacrificial gown.
How can we not think of you in distress?
O how can our heavy heart not sink down?

You find amusement in your lamb's fur dress;
In your fox's fur at court you appear.
How can we not think of you in distress?
O how can our heart not feel sad and drear?

You appear in your greasy dress
Which glistens in the sun.
How can we not think of you in distress?
We are heart-broken at the wrong you've done.

闲暇时你穿着羔羊皮袍多么逍遥，上朝时你狐裘加身仰之弥高。

我怎么可能不思念你？卑微如我，想起来就只是心焦。

闲暇时你穿着羔羊皮袍悠游自在，上朝时你狐裘加身仰之弥高。

我怎么可能不思念你？卑微如我，想起来就只有伤悲。

你的羔羊皮袍润泽如膏，在阳光里光芒闪耀。

我怎么可能不思念你？但卑微如我，想起来只剩哀伤苦恼。

爱一个人，当然是因为对方好。但对方好到一个高度，自己却无法跟从，这种"好"反倒会成为心中的负担。

所以，小人鱼想让王子爱上自己，命运就让王子在最惨的时候遇见她，即便这样阴差阳错间，依旧心事成灰。更不用说诗中女子孤立无援，只能默默地叹息。

桧风·隰有苌楚

隰有苌楚,猗傩其枝。天之沃沃,乐子之无知。
隰有苌楚,猗傩其华。天之沃沃。乐子之无家。
隰有苌楚,猗傩其实。天之沃沃。乐子之无室。

The Unconscious Tree

In lowland grows the cherry
With branches swaying in high glee.
Why do you look so merry?
I envy you, unconscious tree.

In lowland grows the cherry
With flowers blooming in the breeze.
Why do you look so merry?
I envy you quite at your ease.

In lowland grows the cherry
With fruit overloading the tree.
Why do you look so merry?
I envy you from cares so free.

羊桃长在低湿处，枝条繁茂多婀娜。

你永远年轻有光芒，真羡慕你对世上的事知之甚少。

羊桃长在低湿处，花朵如锦多婀娜。

你永远年轻有光芒，真羡慕你不被家庭拖累。

羊桃长在低湿处，果实累累多婀娜。

你永远年轻有光芒，真羡慕你不被家室拖累。

王维有诗曰："木末芙蓉花，山中发红萼。涧户寂无人，纷纷开且落。"看似在说芙蓉花，其实说的是自己心中的理想境界。人生在世，背负太多，倒不如山中树木，只是自在生长。

①猗傩：婀娜。

曹风·候人

彼候人兮,何戈与祋。彼其之子,三百赤芾。

维鹈在梁,不濡其翼。彼其之子,不称其服。

维鹈在梁,不濡其咮。彼其之子,不遂其媾。

荟兮蔚兮,南山朝隮。婉兮娈兮,季女斯饥。

Poor Attendants

Holding halberds and spears,
The attendants escort
The rich three hundred peers,
Wearing red cover-knee in court.

The pelicans catch fish
Without wetting their wings;
The peers have what they wish,
But they're unworthy things.

The pelicans catch fish
Without wetting their beak;
The peers do what they wish,
Unworthy of favor they seek.

At sunrise on south hill
The attendants still wait;
Their hungry daughters feel ill,
Weeping their bitter fate.

守在关口的年轻人,背着戈与棍。

那是谁家子弟?制服加身三百人,他仍然最美。

鹈鹕鸟站在鱼梁上,不肯弄湿它的羽毛。

那是谁家子弟?他迟疑退缩,这可配不上他的衣裳。

醍醐鸟站在鱼梁上,可就尝不到美味了。

那是谁家子弟?他长着一副好皮囊,却还没有将婚姻成就。

云雾弥漫,草木盛大,南山上彩虹升起。

万事万物生机勃勃,我可爱的年轻人,你怎么舍得让那个小姑娘爱而不得。

关于此诗,一说是讽刺庸吏尸位素餐,一说是女孩子讽刺心仪的男子裹足不前。诗无达诂,但从"季女斯饥"看,女孩子多半不会这么形容自己,更像是一个没心没肺的旁观者,抱着胳膊津津有味地看完全过程,对不解风情的年轻人遥遥喊话。

曹风·鸤鸠

鸤鸠在桑,其子七兮。淑人君子,其仪一兮。其仪一兮,心如结兮。

鸤鸠在桑,其子在梅。淑人君子,其带伊丝。其带伊丝,其弁伊骐。

鸤鸠在桑,其子在棘。淑人君子,其仪不忒。其仪不忒,正是四国。

鸤鸠在桑,其子在榛。淑人君子,正是国人。正是国人,胡不万年?

An Ideal Ruler

The cuckoo in the mulberries
Breeds seven fledglings with ease.
An ideal ruler should take care
To deal with all men fair and square.
If he treats all men fair and square,
He would be good beyond compare.

The cuckoo in the mulberries
Breeds fledglings in mume trees.
An ideal ruler should be fair and bright,
His girdle hemmed with silk white.
If he's as bright as silken hems,
He'd be adorned with jade and gems.

The cuckoo in the mulberries
Breeds fledglings in the jujube trees.
An ideal ruler should be polite;
Whatever he does should be right.
If he is right as magistrate,
He'd be a model for the state.

The cuckoo in the mulberries
Breeds fledglings in the hazel trees.
Ruler should be a good magistrate
To help the people of the state.
If he helps people to right the wrong,
May he live ten thousand years loiag!

布谷鸟在桑林里,有七个孩子。

有风度的君子,态度始终如一。

态度始终如一,内心的坚定写在脸上。

布谷鸟在桑林里,它的孩子在梅树上。

有风度的君子,系着素丝带子。

系着素丝带子,皮帽子是青黑色的。

布谷鸟在桑林里,它的孩子落在荆棘树上。

有风度的君子,他的仪容从不改变。

他的仪容从不改变,足以做四方表率。

布谷鸟在桑林里,它的孩子落在榛树上。

有风度的君子,正为国人拥戴。

正为国人拥戴,为什么不能万年永在?

《诗经》里最令人费解的诗之一。传说布谷鸟能够公平对待所有的孩子——当然现在知道这不科学——那么以"鸤鸠在桑"开头，到底在暗示什么呢？

若是说君子当如布谷鸟公平，为什么后来又扯到君子的穿衣戴帽上来？有没有可能，这只是一句随意的起兴？这首诗就是赞扬君子从外到内的坚定？他衣着颜色素朴，仪容始终如一，大家希望他能活一万年。这也许就是一首简单的颂诗。

豳风·伐柯

伐柯如何？匪斧不克。取妻如何？匪媒不得。

伐柯伐柯，其则不远。我觏(gòu)之子，笾豆有践。

An Axe-handle

Do you know how to make
An axe-handle? With an axe keen.
Do you know how to take
A wife? Just ask a go-between.

When a handle is hewed,
The pattern should not be far.
When a maiden is wooed,
See how many betrothal gifts there are.

怎样劈出斧柄？没有斧子可不行。
怎样娶到妻子，离开媒人可不成。

砍斧柄啊砍斧柄，有个样式在手中。
我看见那个姑娘，她把餐具摆得齐整。

这首诗描述的是当时标准的婚姻程序。所谓父母之命、媒妁之言，经媒人说合之后，开始进入全方位考量。笾、豆都是古代食器，是日常礼仪的体现。懂规矩的女子，才是这个特别讲究程序的男子心目中合适的婚姻对象。

豳风·九罭

九罭之鱼,鳟鲂。我觏之子,
衮衣绣裳。
鸿飞遵渚,公归无所,於女信处。
鸿飞遵陆,公归不复,於女信宿。
是以有衮衣兮,无以我公归兮,
无使我心悲兮。

The Duke's Return

In a nine-bagged net
There are breams and red-eyes.
See ducal coronet
And gown on which the broidered dragon flies.

Along the shore the swan's in flight.
Where will our duke alight?
He stops with us only tonight.

The swan's in flight along the track.
Our duke, once gone, will not come back.
His soldiers pass the night in bivouac.

Let's keep his broidered gown.
May he not leave our town
Lest in regret our heart will drown!

渔网孔眼细密,捉住鳟鱼和鲂鱼。

我的这位客人,穿着有龙纹的锦绣衣裳。

鸿雁沿着沙渚飞,您回去我就再也不知道您在哪儿了,不妨在此再宿一晚吧。

鸿雁沿着陆地飞,您回去就不会再回来了,不妨在此处再宿一晚吧。

藏起您那有龙纹的锦绣衣裳,不让您回去啊,不让我的心悲伤啊。

这是一首留客诗,通常认为是下属留他的上司。然而我们细读此诗,也像一个风尘女子,面对即将离去的情人,做出凄婉的挽留。

她如孔眼细密的渔网,向来捕到的都是小鱼;他如昂贵的鳟鱼或鲂鱼,莫名扎了进来。尽管如此,她也知道这露水情缘对他完全没有控制力,一旦他离去,就是永远离去。她只能卑微地求他多住一晚,徒劳地将他绣着龙纹的衣服藏起来。

豳风·狼跋

狼跋其胡,载疐(zhi)其尾。公孙硕肤,赤舄(xì)几几。

狼疐其尾,载跋其胡。公孙硕肤,德音不瑕?

Like an Old Wolf

The duke can't go ahead
Nor at his ease retreat.
He's good to put on slippers red
And leave the regent's seat.

The duke cannot retreat
Nor with ease forward go.
He's good to leave his seat
And keep his fame aglow.

你有没有看到那匹狼？朝前踩到下巴上的肉，朝后绊到自己尾巴上。

公孙你心宽体又胖，一双红鞋穿得真像样。

你有没有见到那匹狼？朝后踩着自己尾巴，朝前撞到自己下巴的肉上。

公孙你心宽体又胖，你的名声肯定很像样。

公孙为谁？我们不得而知，反正就是一个"地主家的傻儿子"，身材肥硕，动作笨拙，偏偏还要穿一双存在感极强的红鞋子。最后说他"德音不瑕"也像是一句讽刺，似乎有"你都这么笨了应该还比较善良吧——不然还有啥亮点呢"的意思。

幽幽 × 南山

第 三 章

CHAPTER THREE
Mountains so long

鹿鸣之什·伐木

伐木丁丁,鸟鸣嘤嘤。出自幽谷,迁于乔木。嘤其鸣矣,求其友声。

相彼鸟矣,犹求友声。矧(shěn)伊人矣,不求友生?神之听之,终和且平。

伐木许许,酾酒有藇(xù)!既有肥羜(zhù),以速诸父。宁适不来,微我弗顾。

於粲洒扫,陈馈八簋(guǐ)。既有肥牡,以速诸舅。宁适不来,微我有咎。

伐木于阪,酾酒有衍。笾豆有践,兄弟无远。民之失德,乾餱(hóu)以愆。

有酒湑我,无酒酤我。坎坎鼓我,蹲蹲舞我。迨我暇矣,饮此湑矣。

Friendship and Kinship

The blows on brushwood go
While the songs of the bird
From the deep vale below
To lofty trees are heard.
Long, long the bird will sing
And for an echo wait;

Even though on the wing,
It tries to seek a mate.
We're more than what it is.
Can we not seek a friend?
If gods listen to this,
There is peace in the end.

Heigh-ho, they fell the wood;
I have strained of my wine.
My fatted lamb is good;
I'll ask kinsmen to dine.
Send them my best regards
Lest they resist my wishes.

Sprinkle and sweep the yards
And arrange eight round dishes.
Since I have fatted meat,
I'll invite kinsmen dear.
Why won't they come to eat?
Can't they find pleasure here?

On brushwood go the blows;
I have strained of my wine.
The dishes stand in rows;
All brethren come to dine.
Men may quarrel o'er food,
O'er late or early brew.

Drink good wine if you could,
Or o'ernight brew will do.
Let us beat drums with pleasure,
And dance to music fine.
Whenever we have leisure,
Let's drink delicious wine.

叮叮当当伐木,嘤嘤咛咛鸟鸣。
鸟儿飞出幽谷,落在高大树巅。
细听它为何鸣叫,原来在寻求友谊之声。

只说这小小的鸟儿,尚求友谊之声。
人乃万物之灵,怎会不求心灵呼应。
还望能谨慎听从,最终和好且平静。

锯木头的声音呼哧哧,滤掉酒糟,这酒多么美。
既然有肥羊,赶紧去请叔叔伯伯们。
凑巧他们不能来,不是我礼节不周到。

盥洗洒扫,窗明几净,摆上佳肴,琳琅满目。
既然有肥牛,赶紧去请各位舅舅。
凑巧他们不能来,不是因为我有过失。

伐木在那山坡上,滤掉酒糟的酒就要满溢出来。
把各种食器都摆好,兄弟们可不要互相疏远。
有些人失了德,为了干粮起争端。

有酒就滤掉酒糟给我饮,没酒就拿那才酿的酒。
鼓儿叮当,舞姿婆娑。
趁着我们这闲暇时刻,喝下这滤过的清澈酒液。

"嘤其鸣矣，求其友声"，是很多邀请函上常用的词句。人生而孤独，对于友谊的渴望却是本能。在农耕社会，这种友谊常存在于亲友之间，虽然说友谊也会带来副产品。比如相距太近，会因酒菜这种细节引发纠纷，但只要用心，相互包容，还是可以避免的。

①神：谨慎。②酤：新酒，一夜酿成的酒，也有译为"买酒"的。

昔我往矣，黍稷方华。今我来思，雨雪载途。
王事多难，不遑启居。岂不怀归？畏此简书。
喓喓草虫，趯趯阜螽。未见君子，忧心忡忡。
既见君子，我心则降。赫赫南仲，薄伐西戎。
春日迟迟，卉木萋萋。仓庚喈喈，采蘩祁祁。
执讯获丑，薄言还归。赫赫南仲，玁狁于夷。

General Nan Zhong and His Wife

Our chariots run
To pasture land.
The Heaven's Son
Gives me command.
Let our men make
Haste to load cart!
The state at stake,
Let's do our part!

Out goes my car
Far from the town.
Adorned flags are
With falcons brown,
Turtles and snakes
They fly in flurry.
O my heart aches
And my men worry.

Ordered am I
To build north wall.
Cars seem to fly
Flags rise and fall.
I'm going forth,
Leading brave sons,
To wall the north
And beat the Huns.

鹿鸣之什·出车

我出我车，于彼牧矣。自天子所，谓我来矣。
召彼仆夫，谓之载矣。王事多难，维其棘矣。
我出我车，于彼郊矣。设此旐矣，建彼旄矣。
彼旟旐斯，胡不旆旆(pèi)？忧心悄悄，仆夫况瘁。
王命南仲，往城于方。出车彭彭，旂旐(zhào)央央。
天子命我，城彼朔方。赫赫南仲，玁(xiǎn)狁(yǔn)于襄。

On parting day
Millet in flower.
On westward way
It snows in shower.
The state at stake,
Can I leave borders?
My heart would ache
At royal orders.

Hear insects sing;
See hoppers spring!
My lord not seen,
My grief is keen.

I see him now;
Grief leaves my brow.
With feats aglow,
He's beat the foe.

Long, long this spring,
Green, green the grasses.
Hear orioles sing;
See busy lasses!
With captive crowd,
Still battle-drest,
My lord looks proud:
He's quelled the west.

我指挥我的车队，在那郊野。
有人从天子那里而来，带来派我出战的消息。
我叫来马夫，叫他把我送到战场。
王事多难，刻不容缓。

我指挥我的车队，在那郊野。
龟蛇旗竖在车上，牦牛尾旗插在两旁。
还有各种旗子，无不迎风飘扬。
而我心中忧虑，车夫亦奔忙到憔悴。

天子命令统帅南仲，在北方的边界筑城抗敌。
车流似云，旗帜招展。
天子命我，筑城于朔方。
南仲威名赫赫，为天子攘除玁狁。

当年我离开家乡，黍稷正是开花时。
如今我踏上归路，满途尽是风雪。
王事多难，我注定要迁徙流离。
我怎会没有归心？就怕忽然收到京城书简。

草丛里虫子一直在叫，蚂蚱爱弹跳。
未见君子，我忧心忡忡。
见到君子，我的心才能止息。
南仲威名赫赫，征伐西戎志在必得。

春日黄昏总是缓慢，花木生长蓁蓁然。
黄鹂鸟喈喈地叫，人们从容地采摘白蒿。
而我在讯问俘虏，怀念故里。
那南仲威名赫赫，玁狁正逐渐平息。

这是一位武士自述他跟随统帅出征及凯旋的诗。从出发，到远征，到筑城迎敌，前面三段写尽战争中的紧张气氛。到了第四段，局面逐渐明朗，作者开始思念家乡。

他想起家乡扬花的黍稷，草丛里的虫声，以及关于爱情的美好。他也想起缓慢的春日里，人们安详地劳作，原本司空见惯的事物，忽然能够标记太平盛世。

鹿鸣之什·杕杜

有杕之杜,有睆其实。王事靡盬,继嗣我日。日月阳止,女心伤止,征夫遑止。

有杕之杜,其叶萋萋。王事靡盬,我心伤悲。卉木萋止,女心悲止,征夫归止!

陟彼北山,言采其杞。王事靡盬,忧我父母。檀车幝幝,四牡痯痯,征夫不远!

匪载匪来,忧心孔疚。期逝不至,而多为恤。卜筮偕止,会言近止,征夫迩止。

A Soldier's Wife

Lonely stands the pear tree
With rich fruit on display.
From the king's affairs not free,
He's busy day by day.
The tenth moon's drawing near,
A soldier's wife, I feel drear,
My husband is not here.

Lonely stands the peat tree;
So lush its leaves appear.
From the king's affairs he's not free;
My heart feels sad and drear.
So lush the plants appear;
A soldier's wife,
I feel drear: Where is my husband dear?

I gather fruit from medlar tree.
Upon the northern hill.
From the king's afairs he's not free;
Our parents rue their fill.
See shabby car appear
With horses weary and drear.
My soldier must be near.

Nor man nor car appear;
My heart feels sad and drear.
Alas! You're overdue.
Can I not long for you?
The fortune-tellers say.
You must be on your way.
But why should you delay?

棠梨树孤单单站立，空有果实累累。

王的事情没完没了，服役的日子不断被延续。

四月已至，女子的心悲伤，征夫啊，你何时才有闲暇？

棠梨树孤单单站立，叶子蔓蔓然面对静寂。

王的事情没完没了，我的心只余伤悲。

世上的花朵都在绽放，女子的心只余伤悲，征夫啊，你何时才能归来？

登上北山，采摘枸杞。

王的事情没完没了，不能不担忧我的父母。

听说连檀木做的车子都已残破，你们的马儿已经疲惫，征夫啊，你应该离我们不远了吧。

没有一辆车，能带他归来，我心中烦恼壅塞。

服役的日子已到期，但你不能归来，我惆怅难解。

我用龟甲和蓍草占卜，得到的都是佳音。

那么见面的日子已经很近了，征夫啊，你离我们越来越近了。

在凄风苦雨中思念亲人固然难以将息，在草长莺飞时想念亲人则更有一种惆怅；所有的生物都在可着劲儿地快乐，只有你没有这种资格。那种被世界遗忘的感觉，让本已经在承受相思之苦的心又雪上加霜。

①阳：四至十月为阳。古时行役，或秋出春归，或春出秋归。看全篇，这里应该是指春天。

南有嘉鱼之什·南有嘉鱼

南有嘉鱼,烝然罩罩。君子有酒,嘉宾式燕以乐。

南有嘉鱼,烝然汕汕。君子有酒,嘉宾式燕以衎。

南有樛木,甘瓠累之。君子有酒,嘉宾式燕绥之。

翩翩者鵻,烝然来思。君子有酒,嘉宾式燕又思。

Southern Fish Fine

Southern fish fine
Swim to and fro.
Our host has wine;
Guests drink and glow.

Southern fish fine
Swim all so free.
Our host has wine;
Guests drink with glee.

South wood is fine
And gourds are sweet.
Our host has wine;
With cheer guests meet.

Birds fly in line
O'er dale and hill.
Our host has wine;
Guests drink their fill.

南方有美好的鱼,成群结队,摇头摆尾。

君子有酒,嘉宾们宴饮多么快乐。

南方有美好的鱼,成群结队,姿态妙曼。

君子有酒,嘉宾们宴饮多么欢喜。

南方的树木枝条下垂,甜葫芦结实累累。

君子有酒,嘉宾们宴饮时光安好。

斑鸠翩翩,结伴而来。

君子有酒,嘉宾们举杯,在宴席上彼此相劝。

君子宴饮嘉宾的场景。通常认为,鱼是餐桌上的美味,这里似乎和结伴而来的斑鸠一样,表现聚会的欢欣。

①烝然:众多。②罩:捕鱼具。罩罩,多貌。③汕汕:鱼游水的样子。

南有嘉鱼之什·南山有台

南山有台,北山有莱。乐只君子,邦家之基。

南山有桑,北山有杨。乐只君子,邦家之光。乐只君子,万寿无疆。

南山有杞,北山有李。乐只君子,民之父母。乐只君子,德音不已。

南山有栲,北山有杻。乐只君子,遐不眉寿。乐只君子,德音是茂。

南山有枸,北山有楰(yú)。乐只君子,遐不黄耇(gǒu)。乐只君子,保艾尔后。

Longevity

Plants grow on southern hill
And on northern grows grass.
Enjoy your fill,
Men of first class.
May you live long
Among the throng!

In south grow mulberries
And in north poplars straight.
Enjoy if you please,
Glory of the State.
May you live long
Among the throng!

Plums grow on southern hill;
On northern medlar trees.
Enjoy your fill,
Lord, as you please.
You're people's friend;
Your fame's no end.

Plants grow on southern hill;
On northern tree on tree.
Enjoy your fill
Of longevity.
You're a good mate
Of our good state.

Trees grow on southern hill
And on northern hill cold.
Enjoy your fill
And live till old.
O may felicity
Fall to posterity!

南山有莎草,北山有藜草。

真高兴我们有位君子,是国家根基。

真高兴我们有位君子,祝您万寿无期。

南山有桑树,北山有杨树。

真高兴我们有位君子,是国家光芒。

真高兴我们有位君子,祝您万寿无疆。

南山有杞柳,北山有李树。

真高兴我们有位君子,堪为百姓之父母。

真高兴我们有位君子,祝您的好名声流传千古。

南山有山樗,北山有檍树。

真高兴我们有位君子,让我们怎能不长寿?

真高兴我们有位君子,您的好名誉像树叶般茂盛。

南山有枳枸,北山有苦楸。

真高兴我们有位君子,让我们怎能不安享晚年。

真高兴我们有位君子,祝您的福泽后世子孙延续。

这是一首颂德祝寿的宴饮诗，也是对君子的颂歌。以树木形容君子，山峰因为有树木而有生机，人世因为有君子而有幸福安宁。

南有嘉鱼之什·菁菁者莪

菁菁者莪,在彼中阿。既见君子,乐且有仪。

菁菁者莪,在彼中沚。既见君子,我心则喜。

菁菁者莪,在彼中陵。既见君子,锡我百朋。

泛泛杨舟,载沉载浮。既见君子,我心则休。

Our Lord Visiting the School

Lush, lush grows southernwood
In the midst of the height.
Now we see our lord good,
We greet him with delight.

Lush, lush grows southernwood
In the midst of the isle.
Now we see our lord good,
Our faces beam with smile.

Lush, lush grows southernwood
In the midst of the hill.
Now we see our lord good,
He gives us shells at will.

The boats of willow wood
Sink or swim east or west.
Now we see our lord good,
Our heart can be at rest.

莪蒿葱茏,生长在山中。

看见那君子,和乐且讲究礼仪。

莪蒿葱茏,生长于小洲。

看见那君子,我心中欢喜。

莪蒿葱茏,生长于土山。

见到君子,胜过赐给我钱财无数。

杨木舟在水中漂荡,时沉时浮。

见到君子,我的心终于可以安宁。

  据说是君子视察学校,太学士因为乐于看到他为国家育才而作此诗。诗中以莪蒿喻人才,青春昂扬,健康成长。而君子对于教育的重视,胜过赏赐万贯钱财,令人感到安慰。

獫狁匪茹，整居焦获。侵镐及方，至于泾阳。
织文鸟章，②白旆央央。元戎十乘，以先启行。
戎车既安，如轾如轩。四牡既佶，既佶且闲。
薄伐猃狁，至于大原。文武吉甫，万邦为宪。
吉甫燕喜，既多受祉。来归自镐，我行永久。
饮御诸友，炰鳖脍鲤。侯谁在矣？张仲孝友。

General Ji Fu

Days in sixth moon are long,
Chariots ready to fight.
All our horses are strong,
Flags and banners in flight.
The Huns come in wild band;
The danger's imminent.
To save our royal land
An expedition's sent.

My four black steeds are strong,
Trained with skill and address.
Days in sixth moon are long;
We've made our battle dress.
Nice battle dress is made;
Each day thirty li's done.
Our forces make a raid,
Ordred by Heaven's Son.

My four steeds are strong ones,
With their heads in harness.
We fight against the Huns
In view of great success.
Careful and strict we'd be;
In battle dress we stand.
In battle dress stand we
To defend the king's land.

The Huns cross the frontier;
Our riverside towns fall.
The invaders come near

南有嘉鱼之什·六月

六月栖栖,戎车既饬。四牡骙骙,载是常服。
玁狁孔炽,我是用急。王于出征,以匡王国。
比物四骊,闲之维则。维此六月,既成我服。
我服既成,于三十里。王于出征,以佐天子。
四牡修广,其大有颙。薄伐玁狁,以奏肤公。
有严有翼,共武之服。共武之服,以定王国。

The chariots move along
And proceed high and low.
The four horses are strong
And at high speed they go.
We fight against the Huns.
As far as northern border.
Wise Ji Fu leads brave sons
And puts the State in order.

North of our capital.
Like flying birds we speed,
With silken flags aglow.
Ten large chariots lead
The way against the foe.

Ji Fu is feasted here
With his gifts on display.
He's back from the frontier,
 Having come a long way.
He entertains his friends
With roast turtles and fish.
The filial Zhang Zhong spends
His time there by Ji's wish.

六月栖栖惶惶,战车准备妥当。
四匹公马雄壮,旗帜车上飘扬。
玁狁气焰嚣张,我方形势急迫。
大王号令出征,匡助我们的王国。

精选四匹黑马,勤训进退有法。
就在这个六月,军装终于制成。
我穿上这军服,当天就走三十里。
大王命令出征,我为天子分忧。

四匹公马健硕,观之高大威武。
我们讨伐玁狁,建立不世之功。
要严肃又恭谨,共同面对战争。
共同面对战争,安定我们的国邦。

玁狁并非等闲,整军于焦获城。
侵袭镐以及方,兵锋直达泾阳。
旌旗绘着飞鸟,帛质的旗帜鲜明。
大战车有十乘,为大军开路先行。

战车既已安妥,不惧路上颠簸。
四匹公马雄健,雄健里透着从容。
我们征伐玁狁,终于抵达大原。
吉甫能文能武,终成万国榜样。

吉甫欢喜赴宴,接受诸多赏赐。
自那镐地归来,我行走了很久。
拿啥宴请诸友,烹煮甲鱼、鲤鱼做脸。
还有谁人与我同在?我的朋友,以孝出名的张仲。

周宣王北伐，尹吉甫从之。这首诗赞美尹吉甫能文能武，同时描述了北伐的全过程。准备出征之初，并没有十足把握，难免惶恐，然而一旦上路，便将气势拉满。尹吉甫严肃地对待战争，恭谨地对待同僚，终于取得胜利，保证了周宣王室的安定，立下赫赫战功。

①栖栖：不安貌，即栖栖惶惶。②白旆：白，通"帛"。白旆：帛质的旗子。

南有嘉鱼之什·吉日

吉日维戊，既伯既祷。田车既好，四牡孔阜。
升彼大阜，从其群丑。
吉日庚午，既差我马。兽之所同，麀鹿麌麌。
漆沮之从，天子之所。
瞻彼中原，其祁孔有。儦儦俟俟，或群或友。
悉率左右，以燕天子。
既张我弓，既挟我矢。发彼小豝，殪此大兕。
以御宾客，且以酌醴。

Royal Hunting

On lucky vernal day
We pray to Steed Divine.
Our chariots in array,
Four horses stand in line.
We come to wooded height
And chase the herds in flight.
Three days after we pray,
Our chosen steeds appear.
We chase all kinds of prey:
Roebucks, does, stags and deer.
We come to riverside.
Where Heavens' Son may ride.

Look to the plain we choose:
There are all kinds of prey,
Here in threes, there in twos,
Now they rush, now they stay.
We chase from left and right.
To the royal delight.
See the king bend his bow,
Put arrow on the string,
On a boar let it go;
A rhino's killed by the king.
He invited guests to dine,
With cups brimful of wine.

戊辰是个吉日,祭拜马神,默默祈祷。
猎车多么好,四匹公马高大威武。
登上那大坡,追逐各种野兽。

庚午也是吉日,挑选我的猎马。
去野兽聚集之地,那里有各种鹿。
顺着漆水与沮水,直到天子之所。

看那中原,猎物何其多。
有的疾飞如电,有的安步当车,成群结伴。
叫左右将其赶出,以令天子开怀。

张开我的弓,拔出我的箭。
射中小野猪,射死大公牛。
拿去宴宾客,美味好下酒。

《红楼梦》里贾母猜灯谜,出谜语的人会悄悄告诉她答案。周王打猎,会有人帮他先去看场地,将野兽赶到一起,让周王狩猎精准,从而有获得感。大人物的快乐就是这么简单。

①儦儦俟俟:儦儦,奔跑。俟俟,慢行。

鸿雁之什·鸿雁

鸿雁于飞,肃肃其羽。之子于征,劬劳于野。
爰及矜人,哀此鳏寡。
鸿雁于飞,集于中泽。之子于垣,百堵皆作。
虽则劬劳,其究安宅?
鸿雁于飞,哀鸣嗷嗷。维此哲人,谓我劬劳。
维彼愚人,谓我宣骄。

The Toilers

Wild geese fly high
With wings a rustling.
We toilers hie
Afield a-bustling.
Some mourn their fate:
They've lost their mate.

Wild geese in flight
In marsh alight.
We build town wall
From spring to fall.
We've done our best
But have no rest.

Wild geese fly high;
They mourn and cry.
The wise may know
Our toil and pain.
The fool says,
"No, Do not complain!"

> 鸿雁飞过，振翅有声。
> 那人正在服劳役，辛苦劳作在旷野。
> 于是想起这世上的可怜人，可怜那些鳏寡之人。
>
> 鸿雁飞过，集于沼泽。
> 那个人在筑墙，百丈的高墙，都是他们在做。
> 虽然很辛苦，但终究是一份安生营生。
>
> 鸿雁飞过，哀鸣嗷嗷。
> 只有那聪明人，知道我辛劳。那些愚蠢的人，
> 把我的悲悯心当成显摆骄傲。

诗人看到鸿雁飞翔，如同人们劳作；见它们停在沼泽中，像人们终于找到一个并不怎么舒服的地方安顿下来；听到它们哀鸣，像是人们发出叹息。聪明人知道悲悯令人痛苦，蠢人还以为他在显摆卖弄。

鸿雁之什·沔水

沔彼流水,朝宗于海。鴥彼飞隼,载飞载止。嗟我兄弟,邦人诸友。莫肯念乱,谁无父母?

沔彼流水,其流汤汤。鴥彼飞隼,载飞载扬。念彼不迹,载起载行。心之忧矣,不可弭忘。

鴥彼飞隼,率彼中陵。民之讹言,宁莫之惩?我友敬矣,谗言其兴。

Water Flows

The waters flow
Towards the ocean.
Hawks fly in slow
Or rapid motion.
My friends and brothers,
Alas! Don't care
For their fathers and mothers
Nor state affair.

The waters flow
In current strong.
Hawks fly now low
Now high and long.
None play their part
But hatch their plot.
What breaks my heart
Can't be forgot.

The waters flow
At rising tide.
Hawks fly so low
Along hillside.
Let's put an end
To talks ill bred,
Respectful friend,
Lest slanders spread.

流水盛大,奔赴海洋。
隼鸟疾飞,时起时停。
感叹我的同姓兄弟,还有我的乡亲与朋友。
还有谁愿意操心这乱世,难道你们没有父母吗?

流水盛大,汹涌而下。
隼鸟疾飞,忽高忽低。
想起那些不守规矩的人,一会儿这样一会儿那样。
我心中的忧伤,无法遗忘。

隼鸟疾飞,沿着那大土山。
民间的讹传,为什么不去制止?
我的朋友啊,你要警惕,当心那谣言兴起。

"知我者谓我心忧,不知我者谓我何求",其他人尚且懵懂,敏感的人已经预感到风暴的来临。他嗅到了崩坏与谣言,竭力去提醒那些醉生梦死的人。然而,言者谆谆,听者藐藐,也只能暗自忧伤。

鸿雁之什·鹤鸣

鹤鸣于九皋,声闻于野。鱼潜在渊,或在于渚。乐彼之园,爰有树檀,其下维萚。它山之石,可以为错。

鹤鸣于九皋,声闻于天。鱼在于渚,或潜在渊。乐彼之园,爰有树檀,其下维榖。它山之石,可以攻玉。

The Crane Cries

In the marsh the crane cries;
Her voice is heard for miles.
Hid in the deep fish lies
Or it swims by the isles
Pleasant a garden's made.
By sandal trees standing still
And small trees in their shade.
Stones from another hill
May be used to polish jade.

In the marsh the crane cries;
Her voice is heard on high.
By the isle the fish lies
Or in tile deep near-by.
Pleasant the garden in our eyes
Where sandal trees stand still
And paper mulberries 'neath them.
Stones from another hill
May be used to polish gem.

鹤鸣于沼泽深处,声音响彻旷野。
鱼潜于深渊,或者游到小洲旁边。
我爱这个园子,园中有高大的檀树,下面落叶堆积。
他山的石头,可以用来磨刀。

鹤鸣于沼泽深处,声音直上云霄。
鱼游到小洲旁边,有时潜入深渊。
我爱这个园子,园中有高大檀树,楮树依它而生。
他山的石头,可以打磨玉器。

你不需要看见鹤,就能感觉到它的存在,它的鸣叫高亢响亮,能从远方传来。高人不需要身在江湖,江湖也不能忽略他的存在;在生长着檀树的园子里,就能够传播自己的声音。就像他山之石,更有一种锋利。

鸿雁之什·白驹

皎皎白驹,食我场苗。絷之维之,以永今朝。所谓伊人,于焉逍遥?

皎皎白驹,食我场藿。絷之维之,以永今夕。所谓伊人,于焉嘉客?

皎皎白驹,贲然来思。尔公尔侯,逸豫无期?慎尔优游,勉尔遁思。

皎皎白驹,在彼空谷。生刍一束,其人如玉。毋① 金玉尔音,而有遐心。

The White Pony

The pony white
Feeds on the hay.
Tether it tight,
Lengthen the joy of the day
So that its master may
At ease here stay.

The pony white
 Feeds on bean leaves.
Tether it tight;
Lengthen the joy of the eves
So that its master may
As guest here stay.

The pony white
 Brings pleasure here.
My noble guest so bright,
Be in good cheer.
Enjoy at ease.
Don't take leave, please!

The pony white
Feeds on fresh grass.
My guest gem-bright.
Leaves, me, alas!
O from you let me hear.
So that to me you're near.

白马皎洁，吃我场上的豆苗。
我绊住它又拴住它，延续和它在一起的时光。
我心里的那个人啊，何妨在此处逍遥。

白马皎洁，吃我场上的豆叶。
我绊住它又拴住它，延续和它在一起的光阴。
我心里的那个人，何妨仍做我的嘉客。

白马皎洁，你光彩照人而来。
何不像一位公侯，安然在此，不存别的期待。
请你慎重斟酌，就此悠游生活，不要遁向远方。

白马皎洁，在远处的空谷。
只需嫩草一束，那个人像玉一样美好。
不要吝惜给我音讯，对我生出疏远之心。

  作者用白马比喻一位无法忘怀的朋友。前面两段可能是写实，这个朋友曾经在作者家中停留过；也可能是想象，作者希望这个朋友能给自己殷勤款待以及挽留的机会。

  然而，白马志在空谷，一束嫩草便能生存。这种无所求的高贵品质，让作者既失落又叹服。

①金玉尔音：将你的声音视为金玉，吝惜音讯之意。

大人占之：维熊维罴，男子之祥；维虺维蛇，女子之祥。

乃生男子，载寝之床。载衣之裳，载弄之璋。其泣喤喤，朱芾斯皇，室家君王。

乃生女子，载寝之地。载衣之裼，载弄之瓦。无非无仪，唯酒食是议，无父母诒罹。

鸿雁之什·斯干

秩秩斯干,幽幽南山。如竹苞矣,如松茂矣。兄及弟矣,式相好矣,无相犹矣。

似续妣祖,筑室百堵,西南其户。爰居爰处,爰笑爰语。

约之阁阁,椓之橐橐。风雨攸除,鸟鼠攸去,君子攸芋。

如跂斯翼,如矢斯棘,如鸟斯革,如翚斯飞,君子攸跻。

殖殖其庭,有觉其楹。哙哙其正,哕哕其冥。君子攸宁。

下莞上簟,乃安斯寝。乃寝乃兴,乃占我梦。吉梦维何?维熊维罴,维虺维蛇。

Installation

The stream so clean,
Mountains so long,
Bamboo so green,
Lush pines so strong.
O brothers dear,
Do love each other.
Make no scheme here
Against your brother.

Inherit all from fathers' tombs,
Build solid wall
And hundred rooms
North, south, east, west.
Where you may walk,
And sit and rest,
And laugh and talk.

The frames' well bound
For earth they pound.
Nor wind nor rain,
Nor bird nor mouse
Could spoil in vain
Your noble house.

As man stands right
As arrow's straight,
As birds in flight
Spread wings so great,
'Tis the abode
Fit for our lord.

Square is the hall
With pillars tall.
The chamber's bright,
The bedroom's deep.
Our lord at night
May rest and sleep.

Bamboo outspread
On rush-mat bed
Where one may rest
Or lie awake
Or have dreams blest
Of bear or snake.

Witches divine
The bear's a sign
Of newborn son
And the snake's one.
Of daughter fine.

When a son's blest
In bed he's laid,
In robe he's drest
And plays with jade.
His cry is loud,
Of crown he's proud,
He'll lord o'er crowd.

When daughter's blest,
She's put aground,
In wrappers drest,
She'll play with spindle round.
She'd do nor wrong nor good
But care for wine and food;
She'd cause her parents dear
Nor woe nor fear.

潺潺清涧，幽幽南山。
有竹苞破土而出，有松树茂密如盖。
住在这里的兄弟，和睦友好，没有怨尤。
继承祖业，营建大片屋舍，朝向南北西东。
于是大家住在一处，终日笑语不息。

你听那咯咯声，是在捆扎木条，你听那橐橐声，是在夯实地基。
待到新屋落成，风雨不来，鸟鼠皆去，君子得以安居。
看那房子，像是有人端正站立，像利箭笔直射出，像鸟儿支棱羽翼，像野鸡即刻飞起。
君子登上台阶，从此在这里起居。

平而正的是那庭院，厅堂前的柱子又高又直。
白天明亮，傍晚昏暗。
君子起居有定，心中多么安宁。

下面是蒲草，上面是竹席，这样的床，让人睡得安心。
一觉醒来，开始回想昨夜的梦。
梦里有啥？有熊有罴，有虺有蛇。

太卜于是来占梦，说有熊有罴，是要生男孩的佳兆；
有虺有蛇，生个女孩会很吉祥。

若是生了男孩，就让他睡小床，就让他穿衣裳，就让他玩玉璋。
他的哭声会很响亮，他穿着华丽的袍服，将来成家立业为君王。

若是生了女孩，就让她睡在地上，用襁褓一包，将纺线的瓦锤交到她手上。
让她不要掺搅是非不要多议多讲，只专心于家中酒食，免得给父母带来非议。

这首诗展现了一个典型的农耕社会场景。在有水草处，偌大的家族聚族而居，约定兄友弟恭，制定男尊女卑的秩序。全诗把叙事、写景、抒情相融合，表现出古代社会对于秩序和血缘关系的无限依赖。

鹿斯之奔，维足伎伎。雉之朝雊，尚求其雌。譬彼坏木，疾用无枝。心之忧矣，宁莫之知？

相彼投兔，尚或先之。行有死人，尚或墐之。君子秉心，维其忍之。心之忧矣，涕既陨之。

君子信谗，如或酬之。君子不惠，不舒究之。伐木掎矣，析薪扡矣。舍彼有罪，予之佗矣。

莫高匪山，莫浚匪泉。君子无易由言，耳属于垣。无逝我梁，无发我笱。我躬不阅，遑恤我后。

节南山之什·小弁

弁彼鸒(yù)斯,归飞提提。民莫不穀,我独于罹。何辜于天?我罪伊何?心之忧矣,云如之何?

踧踧周道,鞠为茂草。我心忧伤,惄焉如捣。假寐永叹,维忧用老。心之忧矣,疢(chèn)如疾首。

维桑与梓,必恭敬止。靡瞻匪父,靡依匪母。不属于毛?不罹于里?天之生我,我辰安在?

菀彼柳斯,鸣蜩嘒嘒,有漼者渊,萑苇淠(pì)淠。譬彼舟流,不知所届,心之忧矣,不遑假寐。

The Banished Prince

With flapping wings the crows
Come back, flying in rows.
All people gay appear;
Alone I'm sad and drear.
O what crime have I even
Committed against Heaven?
With pain my heart's pierced through.
Alas! What can I do?

The highway should be plain,
But it's o'ergrown with grass.
My heart is wound'd with pain
As if I'm pound'd, alas!
Sighing, I lie still dressed;
My grief makes me grow old.
I feel deeply distressed,
Gnawed by headache untold.

The mulberry and other
Trees planted by our mother
And father are protected
As our parents are respected.
Without the fur outside
And the lining inside,
Can we live at a time
Without reason or rhyme?

Lush grow the willow trees.
Cicadas trill at ease.
In water deep and clear
Rushes and reeds appear.

Adrift I'm like a boat;
I know not where I float.
My heart deeply distressed,
In haste I lie down dressed.

The stag of goes
At a fast gait;
The pheasant crows,
Seeking his mate.
The ruined tree
Stript of its leaves
Has saddened me.
Who knows what grieves?

The captured hare
May be released;
The dead o'er there
Buried at least.
The king can't bear
The sight of me;
Laden with care,
My tears flow free.

Slanders believed
As a toast drunk,
The king's deceived,
In thoughts not sunk.
The branch cut down,
They leave the tree.
The guilty let alone,
They impute guilt to me.

Though higher than a mountain
And deeper than a fountain,
The king ne'er speaks light word or jeers,
For even walls have ears.
"Do not remove my dam
And my basket for fish!"
Can't preserve what I am.
What care I for my wish?

寒鸦展翅，群飞回窝巢。

人们看上去都挺好，只有我满心忧愁。

我到底哪里得罪上天？到底有什么罪过？

我心中的忧伤啊，说它又能如何？

大道平坦，周边是丰茂的野草。

我心忧伤，想起来就如有棍子捣。

我闭上眼睛老是叹息，忧伤令人老。

我心中的忧伤啊，燥得让我头疼难消。

见到桑树与梓树，一定会恭恭敬敬。

生为人子，没有不敬重父亲的，没有不依恋母亲的。

如今我不属于外面的裘皮，也不能依附那里子。

老天你让我生下，我的时运又在哪里？

柳枝葳蕤，蝉声嘒嘒。

深渊旁边，芦苇茂密。

就像小舟顺水漂流，不知道该往哪里去。

我心中的忧伤啊,让我没法闭上眼稍稍休息。

鹿儿奔跑,脚步轻捷。

野鸡在早晨鸣叫,寻求它的伴侣。

就像那棵病树,脱落了所有枝条。

我心中的忧伤啊,竟然没有人知道。

看那被捉住的兔子,还有人来放了它。

路上的死人,还有人将他埋葬。

君子的居心,为何如此残忍?

我心中的忧伤啊,让我泪落如雨。

君子听信谗言,就像被敬酒一样舒服。

君子寡恩,不会慢慢地追究真相。

伐木要用绳子拽倒,砍柴要顺着木头纹路。

你把有罪的人放过,却把罪名加到我头上。

不高不能叫山,不深不能叫泉。

君子不要轻易说话,且将耳朵贴在墙上听清楚。

别去管那捕鱼的堤坝,别去动那捉鱼的竹笼。

如今我不被见容,哪里管得了身后的事。

这是一首充满忧愤情绪的哀怨诗。作者受了极大委屈,感觉自己被人们抛弃。作者一连使用五个"心之忧矣",感情沉重,言辞恳切,道尽愁肠百转,然而,他的忧伤并不能得到尊重,只能独自"涕既陨之",极尽幽怨哀伤,零泪悲怀。

荏染柔木，君子树之。往来行言，心焉数之。蛇蛇硕言，出自口矣。巧言如簧，颜之厚矣。

彼何人斯？居河之麋。无拳无勇，职为乱阶。既微且尰，尔勇伊何？为犹将多，尔居徒几何？

节南山之什·巧言

悠悠昊天,曰父母且。无罪无辜,乱如此幠①。昊天已威,予慎无罪。昊天泰幠,予慎无辜。

乱之初生,僭始既涵。乱之又生,君子信谗。君子如怒,乱庶遄沮。君子如祉,乱庶遄已。

君子屡盟,乱是用长。君子信盗,乱是用暴。盗言孔甘,乱是用餤。匪其止共,维王之邛。

奕奕寝庙,君子作之。秩秩大猷,圣人莫之。他人有心,予忖度之。跃跃毚兔,遇犬获之。

Disorder and Slander

O great Heaven on high,
You're called our parent dear.
Why make the guiltless cry
And spread turmoil far and near?
You cause our terror great;
We're worried for the guiltless.
You rule our hapless fate;
We're worried in distress.

Sad disorder comes then
When untruth is received.
Disorder comes again
When slanders are believed.
If we but blame falsehood,
Disorder will decrease.
If we but praise the good,
Disorder soon will cease.

If we make frequent vows,
Disorder will still grow.
If we to thieves make bows,
They will being greater woe.
What they say may be sweet.
The woe grows none the less.
The disorder complete
Will cause the king's distress.

Tha temple's grand,
Erected for ages.
Great work is planned
By kings and sages.

Judge others' mind
But by your own.
The hound can find
Hares running down.

The supple tree
Plant'd by the good,
From slander free.
You can tell truth from falsehood.
Grandiose word
Should not be heard.
Sweet sounding one
Like organ-tongue.
Can deceive none
Except the young.

Who is that knave
On river's border,
Nor strong nor brave,
Root of disorder?
You look uncanny.
How bold are you?
Your plans seem many;
Your followers are few.

悠悠苍天，你是我们的父母。

我们无罪无辜，你降下大难。

苍天你这般发威，我实在是无罪。

苍天你法力无边，我真是无辜之人。

祸乱之初生，是因为谣言一开始就被包容。

祸乱继续弥漫，因为君子信谗。

君子当时若是发怒，祸乱就能快速停止。

君子若能任用贤才，祸乱也许就能彻底结束。

君子总是轻易跟人结盟，祸乱因此生长。

君子相信坏人的话，祸乱于是愈演愈烈。

坏人的话多么悦耳，祸乱于是越来越多。

不是他忠于职守，他危害君王坐下毛病。

宗庙巍峨，君子作之。

了不起的典章，圣人谋划之。

有人生出坏心思，我忖度之。

狡兔跳跃，遇到狗，就被捕获了。

柔弱的小树苗，君子种下。

流言游走，心里哪能分辨。

轻率的大话，出自口矣。

花言巧语，厚颜无耻。

那是怎样的一个人？

居住在河边，没有力气也没有勇气，却给祸乱搭好了台阶。

小腿生疮脚面肿，你的勇气在何处？

阴谋倒是大又多，请问你的同党还有几个？

此诗是一首政治讽喻诗。不同于古诗里常常认为君王被蒙蔽,这首诗直指最高统治者。进谗言者固然可耻,但如果"君子"您能够从一开始就疾言厉色给予惩罚,拨乱反正任用贤良,祸乱很快就会被终结。虽然诗歌的后半部分也斥责了"盗",但最有力量的句子,还是对上天和君子的质问。全诗直抒胸臆,文笔锋利,情感激情酣畅。

①幠:大。②数:辨别。③蛇蛇:通"訑訑",自大貌。④微:小腿生疮。

节南山之什·何人斯

彼何人斯？其心孔艰。胡逝我梁，不入我门？伊谁云从？维暴之云。

二人从行，谁为此祸？胡逝我梁，不入唁我？始者不如今，云不我可。

彼何人斯？胡逝我陈？我闻其声，不见其身。不愧于人？不畏于天？

彼何人斯？其为飘风。胡不自北？胡不自南？胡逝我梁？祇搅我心。

尔之安行，亦不遑舍。尔之亟行，遑脂尔车。壹者之来，云何其盱。

尔还而入，我心易也。还而不入，否难知也。壹者之来，俾我祇也。

伯氏吹埙，仲氏吹篪。及尔如贯，谅不我知，出此三物，以诅尔斯。

为鬼为蜮，则不可得。有靦面目，视人罔极。作此好歌，以极反侧。

Friend or Foe?

Who's the man coming here
So deep and full of hate?
My dame he's coming near.
But enters not my gate.
Is he a follower
Of the tyrant? Yes, sir.

Two friends we did appear;
Alone I am in woes.
My dam he's coming near,
But past my gate he goes.
He is different now;
He has broken his vow.

Who's the man coming here,
Passing before my door?
His voice I only hear,
But see no man of yore.
How can he not fear then
Neither heaven nor men?

Who's the man coming forth
Like a whirlwind which roars?
Why does he not go north
Nor to the southern shores?
Why comes he near my dam
And disturbs what I am?

Even when you walk slow,
You won't stop where you are.
And then when fast you go,
How can you grease your car?
You will not come to see,
Let alone comfort me.

If you should but come in,
Then I would feel at ease.
But you do not come in,
I know you're hard to please.
You won't come to see me,
Nor will set my heart free.

Earthen whistle you blew;
I played bamboo flute long.
When I was friend with you,
We had sung the same song.
Before offerings now,
Can you forget your vow?

I curse you as a ghost,
For you have left no trace.
I will not be your host.
I see your ugly face.
But I sing in distress.
For you are pitiless.

那到底是个什么人？他的心思太难猜。
为何跑到我的鱼梁上去？为什么不进我的门？
他到底听了谁的话？对我这么残忍。

我们携手同行，是谁弄出这祸端？
为何跑到我的鱼梁上去？为什么不来安慰我？
当初他可不这样，如今处处违逆我。

这到底是个什么样的人？为什么从我门前过？
我闻其声，不见其身。
他就不愧于人？他就不畏于天？

这到底是个什么人？就像突然起大风。
为什么不走北边，为什么不走南边？
偏偏到我的鱼梁去，徒乱我心神。

你若是安然向前走，也没空停下休整。
你若是急急向前去，为何停下给车轴上油？
你就这么来一趟，让我眼巴巴地指望。

你回来就进我家门，我的心情就不一样。
你过我家门而不入，我无法将你的心思猜。
你就这么来一趟，使我的心情变舒畅。

大哥吹埙,二哥吹篪。

我们曾经像蚂蚱一条线,到头你是真不懂我。

摆出三物鸡、犬、豕,神前和你发誓盟。

你如果非要做鬼蜮,那么我们就算了。

人有颜面要知愧,我看你完全没准头。

我作这首歌尽是良言,看你还能怎样反复无常。

一个女人的独角戏,她听到他的脚步,以为他就要走进她家门,然后他的脚步远了,徒然乱她心神。在等待的过程中,她内心翻江倒海,想起曾经的爱,酝酿今时的怨,以及怒。爱情有时候很像无实物表演,即使眼前空无一物,也能够自说自话。

节南山之什·巷伯

萋兮斐兮,成是贝锦。彼谮人者,亦已大甚!

哆兮侈兮,成是南箕。彼谮人者,谁适与谋。

缉缉翩翩,谋欲谮人。慎尔言也,谓尔不信。

捷捷幡幡,谋欲谮言。岂不尔受?既其女迁。

骄人好好,劳人草草。苍天苍天,视彼骄人,矜此劳人。

彼谮人者,谁适与谋?取彼谮人,投畀豺虎。豺虎不食,投畀有北。有北不受,投畀有昊!

杨园之道,猗于亩丘。寺人孟子,作为此诗。凡百君子,敬而听之。

A Eunuch's Complaint

A few lines made to be
Fair shell embroidery,
You slanderers in dress
Have gone to great excess.

The Sieve stars in the south
Opening wide their mouth,
You vile slanderers, who
Devise the schemes for you?

You talk so much, o well;
In slander you excel.
Take care of what you say.
Will it be believed? Nay.

You may think you are clever,
Slandering people ever.
But deceived, they will learn
You'll be punished in turn.

The proud are in delight,
The crowd in sorry plight.

Heaven bright, heaven bright!
Look on the proud;
Pity the crowd!

O you vile slanderers,
Who are your counselors?
I would throw you to feed
The wolf's or tiger's greed.
If they refuse to eat,
I'd tread you down my feet
Or cast you to north land
Or throw to Heave's hand.

The eunuch Mengzi, I
Go to the Garden High
By a willowy road long
And make this plaitive song.
Officials on your way,
Hearken to it, I pray.

彩色丝线,织成贝锦。

造谣言者,实在过分。

张开一张大嘴巴,你就成了簸箕星。

造谣言者,谁和你过从?

私语无脚到处飞,想用谣言来害人。

劝你少说几句吧,都说你是不可信的人。

谣言喊喊满天飞,想用谣言来害人。

不是没人上你当,但会反弹到你身上。

骄横的人感觉良好,辛劳的人更加辛劳。

苍天啊苍天,你看看那骄横的人,请怜惜辛劳的人。

那爱造谣的人,谁会和他打交道?

捉住这满嘴瞎话的人,投入豺狼虎豹之中。

豺狼虎豹不食,就投到荒凉的北方。北方也不要,就给他扔到天上!

去杨园的道路,在亩丘上。

我是寺人孟子,写下这首诗,各位君子,请敬而听之。

此孟子非彼孟子也。寺人是小官之名，据说类似于后世的宦官。看前面部分，他写这首诗似乎是被谣言中伤，愤怒出诗人。然而到末尾，又有些劝诫的意思，竟郑重其事地输出人生箴言，可惜他的故事已湮灭不存。但可以推想，必然是小人物会遇到的各种磨难中的一种。

谷风之什·小明

明明上天，照临下土。我征徂西，至于艽野。二月初吉，载离寒暑。
心之忧矣，其毒大苦。念彼共人，涕零如雨。岂不怀归？畏此罪罟！

昔我往矣，①日月方除。曷云其还？岁聿云莫。念我独兮，我事孔庶。
心之忧矣，②惮我不暇。念彼共人，睠睠怀顾！岂不怀归？畏此谴怒。

昔我往矣，日月方奥。曷云其还？政事愈蹙。岁聿云莫，采萧获菽。
心之忧矣，自诒伊戚。念彼共人，兴言出宿。岂不怀归？③畏此反覆。

嗟尔君子，无恒安处。④靖共尔位，⑤⑥正直是与。神之听之，式穀以女。

嗟尔君子，无恒安息。靖共尔位，好是正直。神之听之，介尔景福。

A Nostalgic Official

O Heaven high and bright,
On lower world shed light!
Westward I came by order.
As far as this wild border
Of second month then on the first day;
Now cold and heat have passed away.

Alas! My heart is sad
As poison drives me mad.
I think of those in power;
My tears fall down in shower.
Will I not homeward go?
I fear traps high and low.

When I left home for here
Sun and moon ushered in new year.
Now when may I go home?
Another year will come.
I sigh for I am lonely.
Why am I busy only?

O how can I feel pleasure?
I toil without leisure.
Thinking of those in power,
Can I have happy hour?
Don't I long for parental roof?
I'm afraid of reproof.

When I left for the west,
With warmth the sun and moon were blest.
When can I go home without cares,
Busy on state affairs?
It is late in the year;
They reap beans there and here.

I feel sad and cast down;
I eat the fruit I've sown.
Thinking of those in power,
I rise at early hour.
Will I not homeward go?
I fear returning blow.

Ah! Officials in power,
There's no e'er-blooming flower.
When you're on duty long,
You should know right from wrong.
If Heaven should have ear,
Justice would then appear.

Ah! Officials in power,
There's no e'er-resting hour.
Should you do duty well,
You'd know heaven from hell.
If Heaven should know you,
Blessings would come to view.

上天明朗，照临下方。
我行役去西方，直至边野，满目荒凉。
二月初吉日出发，我已跨越寒冬酷暑。

怎样形容我的忧伤，像毒药那么苦。
想起我的同僚，涕零如雨。
何尝不想归去？害怕触犯法网。

当初我出门，正是辞旧迎新时候。
何时才能归来？看这一年即将过完。
请看我孤单单在路上，可手里的杂事无穷无尽。

我的心多么忧伤，整日辛劳没有闲暇。
想起我的同僚，眷眷怀顾。
何尝不想归去？担心惹来谴责与暴怒。

当初我出门时，天气正变得温暖。
何时才能归来？政事越来越紧促。
眼看一年将尽，家乡正在采收艾蒿和大豆。

我心中的忧伤啊，自寻许多烦恼。
想起我的同僚，我睡不着，起身到外面躺倒。
何尝不想归去？担心将那麻烦找。

唉君子们啊，这世上哪有长久的安宁。
谦恭地守好你的职位，与正直为友。
神明会听到这一切，将美好的生活赐给你。

唉君子们啊，这世上哪有长久的休息。
谦恭地守好你的职位，和正直相亲。
神明会听到这一切，给你盛大的幸福。

古代的征夫，在出差路上，先是感慨自己离家太久，事务繁忙压力大，想起在家乡时的劳作场景，怀念昔日的同僚。但是，他不敢回去，怕惹来麻烦，只好强行给自己灌"心灵鸡汤"，将自己的处境合理化，并期盼苍天给自己一个好结果。这也是大多数人面对重压时的心路历程。

①共人：同僚。②日月方除：旧日辞去，指新年。③反覆：反复，指不测之祸。④靖：敬。⑤共：通"恭"。奉，履行。⑥位：职位，职责。

谷风之什·鼓钟

鼓钟将将,淮水汤汤,忧心且伤。
淑人君子,怀允不忘。

鼓钟喈喈,淮水湝湝,忧心且悲。
淑人君子,其德不回。

鼓钟伐鼛(gāo),淮有三洲,忧心且妯。
淑人君子,其德不犹。

鼓钟钦钦,鼓瑟鼓琴,笙磬同音。
以雅以南,以籥不僭。

Bells and Drums

The bells ring deep and low;
The vast river waves flow.
My heart is full of woe.
How can I forget then
Those music-making men?

The bells sound shrill and high;
The river waves flow by.
My heart heaves long, long sigh.
How can I forget then
Those music-loving men?

The bells and drums resound;
Three isles emerged, once drowned.
My heart feels grief profound.
How can I forget then
Those music-playing men?

They beat drum and ring bell,
Play lute and zither well,
In flute or pipe excel,
Sing odes and southern song
And dance with nothing wrong.

钟鼓锵锵，淮水洋洋，我的心忧愁又悲伤。

善良美好的君子，实在令人难忘。

鼓钟喈喈，淮水洋洋，我的心忧愁又悲伤。

善良美好的君子，德行完美，没有一丝邪僻。

敲起大鼓，在淮上三洲，我的心忧愁又悲伤。

善良美好的君子，德行完美，无可挑剔。

鼓钟钦钦，鼓瑟鼓琴，笙磬相和。

奏《雅乐》也奏《南乐》，籥音也来加入，浑然一体，纹丝不乱。

在礼崩乐坏的时代，想起传说中的君子，会让人感到忧伤。所谓生不逢时，也是其中一种吧。那钟鼓之声，也许是真实的存在，也许是作者的一种想象。他想从想象中的礼乐之声里，回到传统时代，从而既见君子，又感念古代圣贤创造美好音乐的功德。

谷风之什·信南山

信彼南山,维禹甸之。畇畇原隰,曾孙田之。我疆我理,南东其亩。

上天同云,雨雪雰雰,益之以霢霂。既优既渥,既沾既足。生我百谷。

疆埸翼翼,黍稷彧彧。曾孙之穑,以为酒食。畀我尸宾,寿考万年。

中田有庐,疆埸有瓜。是剥是菹,献之皇祖。曾孙寿考,受天之祜。

祭以清酒,从以骍牡,享于祖考。执其鸾刀,以启其毛,取其血膋。

是烝是享,苾苾芬芬。祀事孔明,先祖是皇。报以介福,万寿无疆。

Spring Sacrifice at the Foot of the Southern Mountain

The Southern Mountain stands,
Exploited by Yu's hands.
The plains spread high and low
Tilled by grandsons, crops grow.
Of southeast fields we find
The boundaries defined.

Clouds cover winter sky;
Snowflakes fall from on high.
In spring comes drizzling rain;
It moists and wets the plain.
Fertile grow all the fields;
Abundant are their yields.

Their acres lie in row;
Millet and sorghum grow.
Grandsons reap harvest fine
And make spirits and wine.
They feast their guests with food
That they may live for good.

Gourds grow amid the field
And melons have gross yield.
They are, pickled in slices,
Offered in sacrifices,
That we may receive love
And long life from Heaven above.

We offer purest wine
To ancestors divine;
Kill a bull with red hair
By a knife in hand bare;
We rid it of hair red
And take fat from the bled.

During the sacrifice
The fat burned gives smell nice.
Our ancestors delight
In the service and rite.
We grandsons will be blest
With longest life and best.

终南山绵延,是大禹治理。

原野平整,曾孙耕种。

我划分田界和水渠,开辟出四方田亩。

天上尽是积云,空中雪纷纷,夹杂小雨泠泠。

雨水滋润,水分富足,遂生出百谷。

疆界整齐,黍稷茂密。

曾孙耕种,制成祭奠祖先的酒食。

献给尸神和宾客,保佑我寿考万年。

田中有屋,田边有瓜。

剥掉外皮腌渍,献给我的祖先。

请让曾孙长寿,享受天赐之福。

祭以清酒,再呈上公牛,请祖先享受。

拿起鸾刀,分开牛毛,取出它的血和脂膏。

请享用这冬天的祭品,它们是如此芳香。

祭祀多么有序,先祖请您安享。

请赐我巨大的福报,让我们的生命无限延长。

这是一首周王祭祖祈福的乐歌。古代学者认为曾孙是周王的自称。他首先汇报自己的疆域所在，谈到风调雨顺，再讲到稼穑这生存之根本；中间部分则是叙述了祭奠过程，尤其是祭品的制作，最后希望得到老天赐福。岁末之冬祭是一年农事毕后最后祭奠典，祭歌中着力于歌唱农事来祈来年丰收，亦属自然之事。

甫田之什·甫田

倬彼甫田，岁取十千。我取其陈，食我农人。自古有年。今适南亩，或耘或耔。黍稷薿薿(nǐ)，攸介攸止，烝我髦士。

以我齐明，与我牺羊，以社以方。我田既臧，农夫之庆。琴瑟击鼓，以御田祖。以祈甘雨，以介我稷黍，以穀我士女。

曾孙来止，以其妇子。馌(yè)彼南亩，田畯至喜。攘其左右，尝其旨否。禾易长亩，终善且有。曾孙不怒，农夫克敏。

曾孙之稼，如茨如梁。曾孙之庾，如坻如京。乃求千斯仓，乃求万斯箱。黍稷稻粱，农夫之庆。报以介福，万寿无疆。

Harvest

"Endless extend my boundless fields;
A tenth is levied of their yields.
I take grain from old store
To feed the peasants' mouth.
We've good years as of yore;
I go to acres south.
They gather roots and weed;
Lush grow millets I see.
Collected by those who lead,
They are presented to me.

"I offer millets nice
And rams in sacrifice
To spirits of the land
That lush my fields become.
Joyful my peasants stand;
They play lute and beat drum.
We pray to God of Fields
That rain and sunshine thrives
To increase our millet yields
And bless my men and their wives."

Our lord's grandson comes near.
Our wives and children dear
Bring food to acres south,
The o'erseer opens mouth,
From left to right takes food
And tastes whether it's good.
Abundant millets grow
Over acres high and low.
Our lord's grandson is glad;
His peasants are not bad.

The grandson's crops in piles
Stand high as the roof tiles.
His stacks upon the ground
Look like hillock and mound.
He seeks stores in all parts
And conveys crops in carts.
We peasants sing in praise
Of millet, paddy, maize.
He'll be blessed night and day
And live happy for aye.

田野广阔，每年收获极多。

我只需取出陈粮，就能将治下农夫养活。

自古常是丰年。

今天我去南亩，农夫除草又培土。

黍稷密密簇簇，等它们长大丰收，用以犒赏那些能人。

盛在祭器里的谷物，作为牺牲的羊，都献给你这管土地的四方神。

我田地里的庄稼长得好，这是农人的福分。

我们弹琴鼓瑟又擂鼓，迎接这管农事的田祖。

祈求好雨，滋润我稷黍，养活我这片土地上的男女。

曾孙来到这里，带着妻子和孩子。

送饭给南亩的农夫，管农事的官吏满心欢喜。

礼让他的左右，品尝味道如何。

茁壮的庄稼遍地长，这年必是好收成。

曾孙心满意足，农夫更加卖力。

曾孙的庄稼，堆得像屋顶与桥梁。

曾孙的晒粮场，像小洲与高丘。

还求建千座粮仓，还求建万个车厢。

装满黍稷稻粱，是农夫的好福气。

求神降下大福祉，保佑周朝万寿无疆。

古代君主在春耕时节，会亲自去农田耕地，虽然作秀成分居多，但也表达了对于自然和土地的敬畏。这首诗里的曾孙，通常被认为是君王自己，他一边求神祈雨，一边慰问农人，应该是春耕祭祀时的乐歌。

　　此诗体现了周人对农业生产的重视，表达了先民农耕的辛劳与获得丰收时的快乐。

①攸介攸止：介，大。止，收获。等到长大成熟。②齐明：齐通"粢"。齐明，粢盛，祭祀用的谷物。③克敏：克，能。敏，勤勉。

甫田之什·大田

大田多稼，既种既戒，既备乃事。以我覃耜，俶载南亩。播厥百谷，既庭且硕，曾孙是若。

既方既皁，既坚既好，不稂不莠。去其螟螣，及其蟊贼，无害我田稚。田祖有神，秉畀炎火。

有渰萋萋，兴雨祈祈。雨我公田，遂及我私。彼有不获稚，此有不敛穧，彼有遗秉，此有滞穗，伊寡妇之利。

曾孙来止，以其妇子。馌彼南亩，田畯至喜。来方禋祀，以其骍黑，与其黍稷。以享以祀，以介景福。

Farm Work

Busy with peasants' cares,
Seed selected, tools repaired,
We take our sharp plough-shares
When all is well prepared.
We begin from south field
And sow grain far and wide.
Gross and high grows our yield;
Our lord's grandson's satisfied.

The grain's soft in the ear
And then grows hard and good.
Let nor grass nor weed appear;
Let no insects eat it as food.
All vermins must expire
Lest they should do much harm.
Pray gods to put them in fire
To preserve our good farm.

Clouds gather in the sky;
Rain on public fields come down,
It drizzles from on high
On private fields of our own.
There are unreaped young grain
And some ungathered sheaves,
Handfuls left on the plain
And ears a widow perceives.
And gleans and makes a gain.

Our lord's grandson comes here.
Our wives bring food to acres south
Together with their children dear;
The overseer opens mouth.
We offer sacrifice
With victims black and red,
With millet and with rice.
We pray to fathers dead
That we may be blessed thrice.

大田里多庄稼,一边选种一边修农具,将各样事物都齐备。

用我锋利的犁,松动这南亩。播种百谷,请保佑曾孙平顺。

谷粒始生外壳,渐渐坚实饱满,没有稗子和杂草。

除去各种害虫,不要害我幼苗。

田祖若是有灵,将它们丢进大火。

云起萋萋,好雨密密。

滋润在公田,也惠及私地。

那边有未割的嫩苗,这边有不收的稻谷。

那边有遗漏的禾苗,这边有忘记的谷穗,都是特意给孤苦寡妇的实惠。

曾孙来此,带着妻子和孩子。

送饭给南亩的农夫,管农事的官吏满心欢喜。

曾孙到来时,祭祀正在进行,祭品有黑黄牲口,还有黍和稷。

请享用这些祭品,请赐给我们大福祉。

这首诗可与《甫田》同看,为秋祭之乐歌。展示出一幅远古时代民情风俗和社会生活的生动画卷,表达了民众收获的喜悦,至今仍有重要的认识价值和审美价值。同时,该诗对于缺乏劳动力的寡妇人家也怀有体恤之心。

甫田之什·瞻彼洛矣

瞻彼洛矣，维水泱泱。君子至止，福禄如茨①。

瞻彼洛矣，维水泱泱。韎韐有奭，以作六师。

瞻彼洛矣，维水泱泱。君子至止，鞞琫有珌。

君子万年，保其家室。

瞻彼洛矣，维水泱泱。君子至止，福禄既同。

君子万年，保其家邦。

Grand Review

See River Luo in spring
With water deep and wide.
Thither has come the king,
Happy and dignified,
In red knee-covers new,
Six armies in review.

See River Luo in spring;
Deep and wide flows its stream.
Thither has come the king;
Gems on his scabbard gleam.
May he live long and gay,
His house preserved for aye!

See River Luo in spring;
Its stream flows deep and wide.
Thither has come the king;
He's blessed and dignified.
May he live long and great
And long preserve his state!

请看那洛水，河水恣肆汪洋。
天子来到这里，福禄积攒良多。
兵士们着红色蔽膝，六师精神振作。

请看那洛水，河水恣肆汪洋。
天子来到这里，随身刀鞘多华丽。
愿君子万岁，家室得到保卫。

请看那洛水，河水恣肆汪洋。
天子来到这里，福禄都在他身边汇聚。
愿君子万岁，国家得到保卫。

  朱熹认为，这首诗是天子会见诸侯于东都，讲习武事时，诸侯赞美天子勤于大政的作品。泱泱洛水，雄浑壮阔，寓意天子亲御戎服，威仪崇隆，更可视为天子的精神象征。

①如茨：形容多。

甫田之什·桑扈

交交桑扈,有莺其羽。君子乐胥,受天之祜。

交交桑扈,有莺其领。君子乐胥,万邦之屏。

之屏之翰,百辟为宪。不戢不难,受福不那。

兕觥其觩,旨酒思柔。彼交匪敖,万福来求。

The Royal Toast

Hear the green-beaks' sweet voice
And see their variegated wings fly.
Let all my lords rejoice
And be blessed from on high.

Hear the green-beaks' sweet voice
And see their feather delicate.
Let all my lords rejoice
And be buttress to the state.

Be a buttress or screen,
Set an example fine,
Be self-restrained and keen,
Receive blessings divine.

The cup of rhino horn
Is filled with spirits soft.
Do not feel pride nor scorn,
And blessings will come oft.

青雀鸟交交地叫，华羽闪烁着光泽。
祝君子快乐常有，受到上天的恩宠。

青雀鸟交交地叫，脖颈上的羽毛闪烁光泽。
祝君子快乐常在，您是万邦的屏障。

您是屏障，也是栋梁，是诸侯的榜样。
您克制而守礼，得到的福泽怎么可能不多？

牛角杯弯弯，美酒绵柔。
你不骄横也不傲慢，各种福气自然到来。

这是一首诸侯对君主的赞歌。诸侯既歌颂他的功德光芒，也赞赏他的克制、守礼与温和。此诗多用比喻，语言简洁明快。

鱼藻之什·鱼藻

鱼在在藻,有颁其首。王在在镐,岂乐饮酒。

鱼在在藻,有莘其尾。王在在镐,饮酒乐岂。

鱼在在藻,依于其蒲。王在在镐,有那其居。

The Fish among the Weed

The fish among the weed,
Showing large head, swims with speed
The king in the capital
Drinks happy in the hall.

The fish swims thereamong,
Showing its tail so long.
The king in the capital
Drinks cheerful in the hall.

The fish among the weed
Sheltered by rush and reed,
The king in the capital
Dwells carefree in the hall.

鱼儿游在水藻中,露出它的大脑袋。
天子在那镐京,饮酒作乐多快活。

鱼儿游在水藻中,摇动它长长的尾巴。
天子在那镐京,饮酒作乐多快活。

鱼儿游在水藻中,贴着柔韧的蒲草。
天子在那镐京,安逸地栖居。

用鱼儿的悠游,比喻周王的自在安乐,
讽刺之意很明显了。此诗朴实中寓新奇,其
结构方式和语言技巧,颇似民谣风格。

鱼藻之什·都人士

彼都人士,狐裘黄黄。其容不改,出言有章。行归于周,万民所望。

彼都人士,台笠缁撮。彼君子女,绸直如发。我不见兮,我心不说。

彼都人士,充耳琇实。彼君子女,谓之尹吉。我不见兮,我心苑结。

彼都人士,垂带而厉。彼君子女,卷发如虿(chài)。我不见兮,言从之迈。

匪伊垂之,带则有余。匪伊卷之,发则有旟。我不见兮,云何盱矣。

Men of the Old Capital

Men of old capital
In yellow fox-fur dress,
With face unmoved at all,
Spoke with pleasing address.
At the old capital
They were admired by all.

Men of old capital
Wore their hat up-to-date;
The noble ladies tall
Had hair so thick and straight.
Although I see them not,
Could their face be forgot?

Men of old capital
Wore pendant from the ear;
The noble ladies tall
Were fair without a peer.
Although I see them not,
Could their dress be forgot?

Men of old capital
With girdles hanging down;
And noble ladies tall
With hair like tail of scorpion,
Of them could I see one,
After them I would run.

His girdle hanging there
Suited so well his gown;
Her natural curled hair
Was wavy up and down.
I see not their return.
How much for trem I yearn!

那京都人士，穿着金灿灿的狐皮袍子。

他们神情平静，说话很有章法。

他们的做法总在正道上，是万民仰望的榜样。

那京都人士，戴黑色布帽或者苔草做的斗笠。

那些贵族小姐，头发又密又直。

如今我看不到了，我心中很是郁闷。

那京都人士，冠冕上垂着玉石。

那些贵族小姐，不是姓尹就是姓吉。

如今我看不到了，我心中郁结难消。

那京都人士，衣带飘来飘去。

那些贵族小姐，卷发像上翘的蝎尾。

如今我看不到了，我多想跟她们一起走。

不是她存心要让带子垂下，是那带子实在太长。

不是她存心要把头发卷起，是她的头发原本就弯曲。

如今我看不见她了，我心中多么忧愁。

此诗为周人追思昔日繁盛,悼古伤今之作,一个曾经的"京漂",返乡回想昔日在京都见过的繁华。这繁华具象为昔日京城时髦的贵族男子和小姐,他们代表了最美最先进的时尚,通过描绘他们的衣着、容止和言语等方面,流露出对旧日京都人物仪容的怀念,如今她们已经离开,繁盛成为往事,这使他暗自伤悲。

鱼藻之什·白华

白华菅兮，白茅束兮。之子之远，俾我独兮。

英英白云，露彼菅茅。天步艰难，之子不犹。

滮池北流，浸彼稻田。啸歌伤怀，念彼硕人。

樵彼桑薪，卬烘于煁。维彼硕人，实劳我心。

鼓钟于宫，声闻于外。念子懆懆，视我迈迈。

有鹙在梁，有鹤在林。维彼硕人，实劳我心。

鸳鸯在梁，戢其左翼。之子无良，二三其德。

有扁斯石，履之卑兮。之子之远，俾我疧兮。

The Degraded Queen

White flowered rushes sway
Together with white grass.
My lord sends me away
And leaves me alone, alas!

White clouds with dewdrops spray
Rushes and grass all o'er.
Hard is heavenly way;
My lord loves me no more.

Northward the stream goes by,
Flooding the rice fields there.
With wounded heart I sigh,
Thinking of his mistress fair.

Wood's cut from mulberry tree
To make fire in the stove.
His mistress fair makes me
Lose the heart of my love.

When rings the palace bell,
Its sound is heard without.
When I think of him well,
I hear but angry shout.

The heron may eat fish
While the crane hungry goes.
His mistress has her wish
While I am full of woes.

The lovebirds on the dam
Hide their beaks 'neath left wings.
The woe in which I am
Is what my unkind lord brings.

The stone becomes less thick
On which our feet oft tread.
My heart becomes love-sick
For my lord's left my bed.

菅草开着白花，白茅捆绑着它。
那个人走远了，使我如此孤单。

白云涌起，化为甘霖，滋润菅茅。
时运如此艰难，他又一向无谋。

滮池向北流，滋润稻田。
我啸歌伤怀，惦记着那个高大的人。

砍下桑枝当柴薪，我点燃行灶暖一暖。
想起那个高大的人，实在让我伤心。

宫廷里的钟声，传到宫外。
我念着你，满心忧愁，你看着我，眼神里只有不快。

鹫鸟站在鱼梁上，鹤飞在树林中。
那个高大的人，实在让我伤心。

鸳鸯游在鱼梁，将嘴插进羽翼。
那个人没良心，对我三心二意。

垫脚石扁又扁，遭人踩踏多么卑微。
那个人走远了，让我思念成疾。

这是一首弃妇诗,古代婚姻中的女性处于极不平等的地位,如果遇人不淑,有可能遭遇被遗弃的命运。如同《源氏物语》里的情节,女子被身份高贵的男子抛弃,她面对茫然不知的前途而忧思成疾。诗中的主人公内心既热烈,又卑微凄凉,将自己比喻成垫脚石,但她却无法放弃。

鱼藻之什·绵蛮

①「绵蛮黄鸟,止于丘阿。道之云远,我劳如何。」「饮之食之,教之诲之。

命彼后车,谓之载之。」

「绵蛮黄鸟,止于丘隅。岂敢惮行,畏不能趋。」「饮之食之,教之诲之。

命彼后车,谓之载之。」

「绵蛮黄鸟,止于丘侧。岂敢惮行,畏不能极。」「饮之食之,教之诲之。

命彼后车,谓之载之。」

Hard Journey

O hear the oriole's song!
It rests on mountain slope.
The journey's hard and long.
How can a tired man cope?
Give me food and be kind,
Help me, encourage me,
Tell the carriage behind
To stop and carry me!

O hear the oriole's song!
It rests at mountain yon.
Do I fear journey long?
I fear I can't go on.
Give me food and be kind,
Help me, encourage me,
Tell the carriage behind
To stop and carry me!

O hear the oriole's song!
 It rests at mountain's bend.
Do I fear journey long?
I can't get to its end.
Give me food and be kind,
Help me, encourage me,
Tell the carriage behind.
To stop and carry me!

"小小黄鸟,停在远处的山丘。道路遥远,我实在是辛劳。"

"给他水和食物,教他一点自救之道。告诉后面的车夫,载上这个疲惫不堪的人。"

"小小黄鸟,停在山坡上的角落。哪里敢畏惧行走?只是怕走得太慢。"

"给他水和食物,教他一点自救之道。告诉后面的车夫,载上这个疲惫不堪的人。"

"小小黄鸟,停在山坡一侧。哪里敢害怕行走?只是担心不能到达。"

"给他水和食物,教他一点自救之道。告诉后面的车夫,载上这个疲惫不堪的人。"

这首诗很像影视剧里的场景，行役者望着远处山坡上的黄鸟，那里可能是他心里暂时给自己定的目标，但非常遥远，他觉得自己很难抵达。

行役者的疲惫被一个坐车的人看在眼里，此人同理心很强，愿意从物质和精神上给予他鼓励。

虽然说命运很难改变，但小小的善意也是我们在人生这条行役之路上走下去的精神动力。

---

①绵蛮：形容鸟小，也有说形容鸟啼，或者鸟羽毛纹路如锦。

鱼藻之什·渐渐之石

渐渐之石,维其高矣。山川悠远,维其劳矣。①
武人东征,不皇朝矣。②

渐渐之石,维其卒矣。山川悠远,曷其没矣?
武人东征,不皇出矣。

有豕白蹢,烝涉波矣。月离于毕,③俾滂沱矣。④
武人东征,不皇他矣。

Eastern Expedition

The mountain frowns
With rocky crowns.
Peaks high, streams long,
Toilsome the throng.
Warriors east go;
No rest they know.

The mountain frowns
With craggy crowns.
Peaks high, streams bend.
When is the end?
Warriors go east.
When be released?

White-legged swines wade
Through streams and fade.
In Hyades the moon.
Foretells hard rain soon.
Warriors east go;
No plaint they show.

巍巍山石，何其高矣。
山川悠远，何其辽矣。
将士东征，没有时间休息。

巍巍山石，何其险矣。
山川悠远，尽头在哪里？
将士东征，没时间考虑安危。

白蹄小猪，挤在一起涉水。
月亮靠近毕星，将使大雨滂沱。
将士东征，想不到其他的了。

    这是一首记述将士东征途中劳苦之情的诗歌。说是没有闲暇考虑安危，实际上这些将士可能也不想考虑安危。在没有选择的情况下，将士们想得越多就越痛苦。他们不顾早晚，不畏艰辛，无思无虑地朝前赶路，纵然知道即将大雨滂沱，也只能咬紧牙关，勇敢前进。

①旁：广阔。②皇：闲暇。③离：附丽，依附。④毕：星宿名，毕星。

鱼藻之什·何草不黄

何草不黄?何日不行?何人不将?经营四方。

何草不玄?何人不矜?哀我征夫,独为匪民。

匪兕匪虎,率彼旷野。哀我征夫,朝夕不暇。

有芃者狐,率彼幽草。有栈之车,行彼周道。

Nowhere but Yellow Grass

Nowhere but yellow grass,
Not a day when we've rest,
No soldier but should pass
Here and there, east or west.

Nowhere but rotten grass,
None but has left his wife,
We poor soldiers, alas!
Lead an inhuman life.

We're not tigers nor beast.
Why in the wilds do we stay?
Alas! We're men at least.
Why toil we night and day?

Unlike the long-tailed foxes
Deep hidden in the grass,
In our carts with our boxes
We toil our way, alas!

哪一棵草不曾枯黄？哪一天我不行走在路上？

哪个人可以不服役，我到处经营，四方奔忙。

哪一棵草不曾焦黑？哪一个人完全健全？

可怜我这征夫，唯独不被当人。

不是野牛不是虎，为什么走在这旷野上？

可怜我这征夫，从早到晚没有闲暇。

狐狸尾巴蓬松松，一头钻进幽草中。

看那役车高又大，昂然走在那大道上。

宋代朱熹在《诗集传》中评说此诗："周室将亡，征役不息，行者苦之，故作此诗。"一个被生活碾压的行役者，为了公事奔走四方，他看所有的风景都是萧索，感觉自己犹如野兽，是非人类的存在。而役车高大，只顾走在既定的道路上，不会对这个呼天吁地的人有一丝悲悯。本诗中采用多处反问句式来诉说征夫所过的非人生活，接连五个"何"字句的责问，是行役者痛苦的泣诉和满腔的愤懑，也是对统治者强烈的抗议，"哀我征夫，独为匪民"，此句更是感情强烈，直揭主题。

①矜：瘝，病。另一说为"鳏"。②栈：役车高高的样子。

绵绵瓜瓞

第四章

CHAPTER FOUR

Gourds grow in long, long trains

侯服于周，天命靡常。殷士肤敏，祼将于京。厥作祼将，常服黼冔xú。王之荩jin臣，

无念尔祖。

无念尔祖，聿修厥德。永言配命，自求多福。殷之未丧师，克配上帝。宜鉴于殷，

骏命不易！

命之不易，无遏尔躬。宣昭义问，有虞殷自天。上天之载，无声无臭。仪刑文王，

万邦作孚。

文王之什·文王

文王在上，於昭于天。周虽旧邦，其命维新。有周不显，帝命①不时。文王陟降，在帝左右。

亹wěi亹文王，令闻不已。陈锡哉周，侯文王孙子。文王孙子，本支百世，凡周之士，不显亦世。

世之不显，厥犹翼翼。思皇多士，生此王国。王国克生，维周之桢；济济多士，文王以宁。

穆穆文王，於缉熙敬止。②假哉天命，有商孙子。商之孙子，其丽不亿。上帝既命，侯于周服。

Heavens Decree

King Wen rests in the sky;
His spirit shines on high.
Though Zhou is an old state,
It's destined to be great.
The House of Zhou is bright;
God brings it to the height.
King Wen will e'er abide
At God's left or right side.

King Wen was good and strong;
His fame lasts wide and long.
God's gifts to Zhou will run
From his son to grandson.
Descendants of his line
Will receive gifts divine;
So will talents and sage
Be blessed from age to age;

From age to age they're blest;
They work with care and zest.
Brilliant, they dedicate
Their lives to royal state.
Born in this royal land,
They'll support the house grand.
With talents standing by,
King Wen may rest on high.

King Wen was dignified,
Respected far and wide.
At Heaven's holy call
The sons of Shang come all.

Those sons of the noblesse
Of Shang are numberless.
As heaven orders it,
They cannot but submit.

Submission's nothing strange;
Heaven's decree may change.
They were Shang's officers;
They're now Zhou's servitors.
They serve wine in distress
In Shang cap and Yin dress.
You loyal ministers,
Don't miss your ancestors!

Miss no ancestors dear;
Cultivate virtue here!
Obey Heaven's decree
And you'll live in high glee.
Ere it lost people's heart,
Yin played its ordained part.
From Yin's example we see
It's hard to keep decree.

O keep Heaven's decree
Or you will cease to be.
Let virtue radiate;
Profit from Yin's sad fate:
All grow under the sky
Silently far and nigh.
Take pattern from King Wen.
All states will obey you then.

文王在上，上天已经昭明。

周虽是旧邦，使命却是革新。

周的未来显赫，上天之命正确。

文王无论起落，都在上天左右。

文王勤勉，美名不息。

给周朝带来莫大福利，惠及文王的子孙。

文王子孙，本宗与旁支都延续百世。

但凡周的宗族，都能够世代显赫。

世代显赫，需要小心筹划。

有那么多杰出之士，生在这个国家。

国家诞生这么多能人，都是周的栋梁。

人才济济，文王就能安宁。

温和庄重的文王，光明磊落又敬畏上天。

天命多伟大，不妨看看商的子孙。

商的子孙，无穷无尽。

上天既然有命，就臣服于周。

臣服于周，接受天命无常。

殷的旧臣美好聪敏，来京城参加祼祭典礼。

他们行灌祭之礼，穿旧时衣冠。

为王尽忠的臣子，怎能不念你的祖先。

怎能不念你的祖先，修行美好的品德。

永远配合天命，自求多福。

殷当年没有丧失民心，也能与天意相称。

应该以殷为鉴，持有大命可不易。

持有大命不易，不要在你们身上断绝。

布播文王美名，也要考虑殷的兴废取决于上天。

上天行事，无声无息无气味，不可猜度。

只要效仿文王，那么万邦就会相信你。

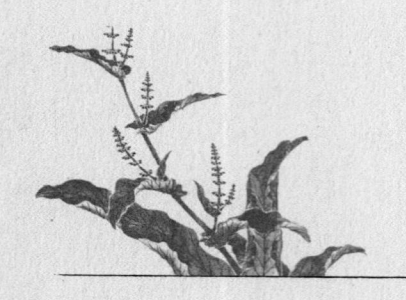

此诗描写的是周王朝在祭祀、朝会等盛典时期对周文王的歌颂与赞美，诗句恳切叮咛，理正情深，是文王的颂歌中思想与语言艺术方面都较为成功的一篇。诗篇旨在阐述：文王得天下不只是因为他有美好的品德，更因为他受命于天。这使得文王的权力顺应天意，更加不能撼动。至于说这个天意是什么样的，无法猜度，总之大家跟从文王就好了，就会有好的结果。

①不时："不"通"丕"，大。"时"通"是"。②假：伟大。③荩臣：忠臣。

有命自天,命此文王。于周于京,缵女维莘。长子维行,笃生武王。保右命尔,燮伐大商。

殷商之旅,其会如林。矢于牧野,维予侯兴。上帝临女,无贰尔心。

牧野洋洋,檀车煌煌,驷𫘤彭彭。维师尚父,时维鹰扬。凉彼武王,肆伐大商,会朝清明。

文王之什·大明

明明在下,赫赫在上。天难忱斯,不易维王。天位殷适,使不挟四方。

挚仲氏任,自彼殷商,来嫁于周,曰嫔于京。乃及王季,维德之行。

大任有身,生此文王。维此文王,小心翼翼。昭事上帝,聿怀多福。厥德不回,以受方国。

天监在下,有命既集。文王初载,天作之合。在洽之阳,在渭之涘。

文王嘉止,大邦有子。大邦有子,伣天之妹。文定厥祥,亲迎于渭。造舟为梁,不显其光。

Three Kings of Zhou

Gods know on high
What's done below.
We can't rely
On grace they show.
It's hard to retain
The royal crown.
Yin-shang did reign;
It's overthrown.

Ren, Princess Yin,
Left Shang's town-wall
To marry in Zhou's capital.
She wed King Ji,
The best of men.

Then pregnant, she
Gave birth to Wen.
When he was crowned,
Wen served with care
The gods around,
Blessed here and there.
His virtue's great,
Fit head of the state.

Heaven above.
Ruled o'er our fate.
It chose with love
For Wen a mate.
On sunny side
Of River Wei

Wen found his bride
In rich array.
Born in a large state,
The celestial bride
And auspicious mate
Stood by riverside.
On bridge of boats they met,
Splendor ne'er to forget.

At Heaven's call
Wen again wed in capital
Xin nobly-bred.
She bore a son
Who should take down,
When victory's won,
The royal crown.

Shang troops did wield
Stones on hard wood.
Wu vowed afield:
 "To us kinghood!
Gods are behind.
Keep your strong mind!"

The field is wide;
War chariots strong.
The steeds we ride
Gallop along.
Our Master Jiang
Assists the king

* 198

To overthrow the Shang
Like eagle on the wing.
A morning bright
Displaced the night.

德行在下,天命在上。

天命向来难信,为人君也不容易。

天子之位也曾适合殷嗣,上天也能让他失去四方。

挚国任家的二女儿,从那殷商,来嫁于周,成为京都新娘。

她与王季携手,推行良善主张。

任氏怀有身孕,生下这位文王。

这位文王,小心翼翼。

明白怎样侍奉上天,引来福泽和吉祥。

他的品德纯粹无邪,凭此吸引四方来附之国。

老天看着下方,文王接受这天命。

文王刚刚即位,便有天作之合。

在洽河之北,在渭水之泮。

文王举行婚礼，大邦莘国有个好姑娘。

大邦莘国有个好姑娘，美如天仙好模样。

占卜得吉送聘礼，亲迎直到渭水旁。

连接小舟为桥梁，这场婚礼好风光。

有命自天，交付文王，在周之京都。

莘国这美好的女子，她是家中长女，婚后生下武王。

老天保之佑之命之，让他袭伐殷商。

殷商之旅，旌旗如林。

武王起誓于牧野：我即将兴起。上天正在看着你们，你们要对我一心一意。

牧野广阔，檀车煌煌，马匹强壮。

统帅尚父，若雄鹰飞扬。

他辅佐那武王，纵兵讨伐殷商，会战于早晨，开启清明气象。

但凡一个人成功了，必然要追溯到他的祖上。这首诗从文王的父母开始赞美，再到他的婚姻，阐述他的成功具有必然性；再讲述他讨伐殷商、决战牧野等一系列丰功伟绩，塑造出文王功高德明的伟大形象。此诗规模宏大，结构严谨，是周部族的史诗性颂诗。

①回：邪僻。②会：旌旗。

肆不殄厥愠,亦不陨厥问。柞棫拔矣,行道兑矣。混夷駾矣,维其喙矣!

虞芮质厥成,文王蹶厥生。予曰有疏附,予曰有先后。予曰有奔奏,予曰有御侮!

文王之什·绵

绵绵瓜瓞(dié)。民之初生,自土沮漆。古公亶父,陶复陶穴,未有家室。

古公亶父,来朝走马。率西水浒,至于岐下。爰及姜女,聿来胥宇。

周原膴膴,堇荼如饴。爰始爰谋,爰契我龟,曰止曰时,筑室于兹。

乃慰乃止,乃左乃右,乃疆乃理,乃宣乃亩。自西徂东,周爰执事。

乃召司空,乃召司徒,俾立室家。其绳则直,缩版以载,作庙翼翼。

捄之陾陾(réng),度之薨薨,筑之登登,削屡冯冯。百堵皆兴,鼛(gāo)鼓弗胜。

乃立皋门,皋门有伉。乃立应门,应门将将。乃立冢土,戎丑攸行。

The Migration in 1325 B. C.

Gourds grow in long, long trains;
Our people grew in the plains.
They moved to Qi from Tu,
Led by old Duke Tan Fu,
And built kiln like hut and cave
For house they did not have.

Tan Fu took morning ride
Along the western side.
Of River Wei came he
To the foot of Mount Qi;
His wife Jiang came at his right
To find a housing site.

Zhou plain spread at his feet
With plants and violets sweet.
He asked his men their mind,
And by tortoise shell divined.
He was told them to stay
And build homes right away.

They settled at the site
And planned to build left and right.
They divided the ground
And dug ditches around.
From west to east there was no land
But Tan Fu took in hand.

He named two officers
In charge of laborers
To build their houses fine.
They made walls straight with the line
And bound the frame-boards tight.
A temple rose in sight.

They brought basketfuls of earth
And cast it in frames with mirth.
Then they beat it with blows
And pared the walls in rows.
A hundred walls did rise;
Drums were drowned in their cries.

They set up city gate;
It stood so high and straight.
They set up palace door
They'd never seen before.
They reared an altar grand.
To spirits of the land.

The angry foe not tame
Feared our Duke Tan Fu's name.
Oaks and thorns cleared away,
People might go their way.
The savage hordes in flight
Panted and raft out of sight.

The lords no longer strove;
King Wen taught them to love.
E'en strangers became kind;
They followed him behind.
He let all people speak
And defended the weak.

大瓜小瓜,绵绵不绝。

民之初生,自杜到漆。

古公亶父,挖完土窑挖土穴,没有屋舍。

古公亶父,快马避乱。

顺着渭水边往西走,一直来到岐山下。

于是协同妻子太姜,相看地形要落脚。

周原肥沃,乌头菜与苦菜甘甜。

大家开始谋划,刻龟甲占卜吉凶。

说这个地方可以居停,便筑室于兹。

安心住在此地,将周围土地开垦。

画出大界分田块,疏导沟渠治田畴。

从西到东连成片,所有人齐上阵。

乃召司空,乃召司徒,让他们去建房。

拉开绳墨画直线,束起夹板稳地基,建起这庙宇何其庄严。

盛土声陾陾，倒土声薨薨，筑墙声登登，削治声冯冯。

无数墙建起，那宏大的声音，大鼓都不能更胜一筹。

建起正城门，正城门多高大。
建起王宫门，王宫门多庄正。
建起大社，大家一同前去祈祷。

直到今天狄人仍怒气不绝，但这并不损害文王的声誉。
柞树棫树都拔掉，终于有通达的大道。
混夷溃败奔突，喘息不定。

虞芮两国平和，是文王将他们感动。
我有贤臣奔赴，我有良臣辅佐左右。
我有文臣传播美名，我有武臣可以御侮。

这是周部族的史诗性颂诗，气韵贯通，感情丰沛，将文王的功业追根溯源，直至他的祖父古公亶父。他原本避乱而来，在这风水宝地安营扎寨，修筑城池。后世像大瓜小瓜般绵延不绝，励精图治，终于有了今天这样八方来朝的气象。此诗以时间为经，以地点为纬，景随情迁，情随景发，流露出周人乐享生活、热爱生命、崇敬祖先的真挚情感。

①缩版：缩，困束。版，夹土的木板，做墙之用。

文王之什·棫朴

芃芃棫朴,
薪之槱之。
济济辟王,
左右趣之。

济济辟王,
左右奉璋。
奉璋峨峨,
髦士攸宜。

淠彼泾舟,
烝徒楫之。
周王于迈,
六师及之。

倬彼云汉,
为章于天。
周王寿考,
遐不作人?

追琢其章,
金玉其相。
勉勉我王,
纲纪四方。

King Wen and Talents

Oak trees and shrubs lush grow;
They'll make firewood in row.
King Wen has talents bright
To serve him left and right.

King Wen has talents bright
To hold cups left and right.
To offer sacrifice
And pour libations nice,

On River Jin afloat
Many a ship and boat.
The king orders to fight
Six hosts of warriors bright.

The Milky Way on high
Makes figures in the sky.
The king of Zhou lives long
And breeds talents in throng.

Figures by chisels made
Look like metal or jade.
With them our good king reigns
Over his four domains.

械树朴树皆茂盛,伐作柴薪堆成堆。
容貌丰美我文王,贤臣跟在他左右。

容貌丰美我文王,左右跟随捧圭璋。
捧璋臣子多轩昂,俊美之士都很强。

舟行于泾水,众人划桨。
周王出征,六师跟从。

银河浩渺,天上华章。
周王高寿,人才怎会没有长远眼光。

外表雕花,金玉在里。
我王勤勉,纲纪立于四方。

  这是歌颂周文王领兵伐崇的诗。极力赞美文王善于用人,以德服人。朱熹认为,"前三章言文王之德,为人所归;后二章言文王之德,有以振作纲纪天下之人,而人归之"。

文王之什·旱麓

瞻彼旱麓，榛楛济济。岂弟君子，干禄岂弟。

瑟彼玉瓒，黄流在中。岂弟君子，福禄攸降。

鸢飞戾天，鱼跃于渊。岂弟君子，遐不作人？

清酒既载，骍牡既备。以享以祀，以介景福。

瑟彼柞棫，民所燎矣。岂弟君子，神所劳矣。

莫莫葛藟，施于条枚。岂弟君子，求福不回。

Sacrifice and Blessing

At the mountain's foot, lo!
How lush the hazels grow!
Our prince is self-possessed
And he prays to be blessed.
The cup of jade is fine,
O'erflowed with yellow wine.
Our prince is self-possessed;
He prays and he is blessed.
The hawks fly in the sky;
The fish leap in the deep.
Our prince is self-possessed;
He prays his men be blessed.

Jade cups of wine are full;
Ready is the red bull.
He pays the sacred rite
To increase blessings bright.
Oaks grow in neighborhood,
And are used for firewood.
Our prince is self-possessed;
By gods he's cheered and blessed.
How the creeper and vine
Around the branches twine!
Our prince is self-possessed;
He prays right and is blessed.

遥望旱山麓，榛楛密密生。
君子常和乐，和乐求福气。

圭瓒多莹洁，美酒在其中。
和乐之君子，福禄自垂青。

苍鹰飞上天，鱼儿跃于渊。
和乐之君子，培养后来人。

清酒已在樽，祭牲也备齐。
上供祭祖宗，祈福向神灵。

柞棫密密生，砍下拿火烧。
和乐之君子，神灵必慰劳。

葛藤长而软，缠绕到树梢。
和乐之君子，不将祖宗违。

此诗描写了君子（或周文王）祭祀以求福。君子多和乐，因为温和才能清醒，清醒才能洞明；能够看清自己和他人，必然会获得福分。当然，这首诗写的还是祭祀的场景，将和乐之人的福分，归结为神灵保佑。

①岂弟：温和，平易近人。

诞后稷之穑,有相之道。茀厥丰草,种之黄茂。实方实苞,实种实褎。实发实秀,实坚实好。实颖实栗,即有邰家室。

诞降嘉种,维秬维秠,维穈维芑。恒之秬秠,是获是亩。恒之穈芑,是任是负,以归肇祀。

诞我祀如何?或舂或揄,或簸或蹂。释之叟叟,烝之浮浮。载谋载惟,取萧祭脂。

诞我祀如何?取羝以軷③,载燔载烈,以兴嗣岁。

卬盛于豆,于豆于登,其香始升。上帝居歆,胡臭亶时。后稷肇祀,庶无罪悔,以迄于今。

生民之什·生民

厥初生民,时维姜嫄。生民如何?克禋克祀,以弗无子。履帝武敏歆,攸介攸止，

载震载夙。载生载育,时维后稷。

诞弥厥月,先生如达。不坼不副,无菑无害,以赫厥灵。上帝不宁,不康禋祀,居然生子。

诞寘之隘巷,牛羊腓字之。诞寘之平林,会伐平林。诞寘之寒冰,鸟覆翼之。

鸟乃去矣,后稷呱矣。实覃实訏,厥声载路。

诞实匍匐,克岐克嶷,以就口食。蓺之荏菽,荏菽旆旆。禾役穟穟,麻麦幪幪，

瓜瓞唪唪。

Hou Ji, the Lord of Corn

Who gave birth to the Lord of Corn?
By Lady Jiang Yuan he was born.
How gave she birth to her son nice?
She went afield for sacrifice.
Childless, she prayed for a son, so
She trod on the print of God's toe.
She stood there long and took a rest,
And she was magnified and blessed.
Then she conceived, then she gave birth,
It was the Lord of Corn on earth.

When her carrying time was done,
Like a lamb slipped down her first son.
Of labor she suffered no pain;
She was not hurt, nor did she strain.
How could his birth so wonderful be?
Was it against Heaven's decree?
Was God displeased with her sacrifice.

To give a virgin a son nice?
The son abandoned in a lane
Was milked by the cow or sheep.
Abandoned in a wooded plain,
He's fed by men in forest deep.
Abandoned on the coldest ice,
He was warmed by birds with their wings.
When flew away those birds so nice,
The cry was heard of the nursling's.
He cried and wailed so long and loud
The road with his voice was o'erflowed.

He was able to crawl aground.

And then rose to his feet.
When he sought food around,
He learned to plant large beans and wheat.
The beans he planted grew tall;
His millet grew in rows;
His gourds teemed large and small;
His hemp grew thick and close.

The Lord of Corn knew well the way
To help the growing of the grain.
He cleared the grasses rank away
And sowed with yellow seed the plain.
The new buds began to appear;
They sprang up, grew under the feet.
They flowered and came into ear;
They drooped down, each grain complete.
They became so good and so strong,
Our Lord would live at Tai for long.

Heaven gave them the lucky grains
Of double-kernelled millet black
And red and white ones on the plains,
Black millet reaped was piled in stack.
Or carried back on shoulders bare.
Red and white millet growing nice
And reaped far and wide, here and there,
Was brought home for the sacrifice.

What is our sacrifice?
We hull and ladle rice,
We sift and tread the grain,
Swill and scour it again.

It's steamed and then distilled;
We see the rites fulfilled.
We offer fat with southern wood.
And a skinned ram as food.
Flesh roast or broiled with cheer.
Brings good harvest next year.

We load the stands with food,
The stands of earthenware or wood.
God smells its fragrance rise;
He's well pleased in the skies.
What smell is this, so nice?
It's Lord of Corn's sacrifice.
This is a winning way;
It's come down to this day.

　　当初周民诞生，姜嫄就是祖宗。

　　周氏如何诞生，以禋祭礼向上天求乞，免我无子之灾。

　　踩着上天足迹而有感，等待瓜熟蒂落，庄重对待孕事，然后顺利生育，便是这个后稷。

　　十月怀胎，头胎像小羊带着胞衣，不破也不裂，没有灾也没有害，以显示神迹发生。

　　好似上帝不肯安宁，不能够享受禋祀，所以产下此子。

　　把他扔到狭窄的巷子中，牛羊庇护他。

　　把他丢到树林里，碰到伐木人收留了他。

把他扔到寒冰上,鸟儿用羽毛覆盖他。

等到鸟儿离去,后稷放声啼哭。

哭声悠长响亮,回荡在道路上。

待他能匍匐爬行,已经伶俐聪明,能够找到食物,放入自己口中。

稍大就能种豆,豆子长得密又高。

禾穗长得漂亮,麻麦更是繁茂。

还有大瓜小瓜,多得吃不了。

后稷稼穑,辨识物种有门道。

拔除丰茂的杂草,庄稼就能长好。

它们发芽打苞,它们渐渐长高,它们抽条结穗,它们的果实很饱,它们禾穗累累,沉沉往下坠。

这丰功伟绩得到奖励,尧将邰地封给后稷为家。

老天赐予好种子,有秬有秠,有穈有芑。

秬秠种满地,割下堆田里。

穈芑种满地,又挑又抱送家里,用以肇祀。

我们的祭祀什么样?

有人臼米有人舀起,有人簸糠有人搓皮。

淘米声嗖嗖,蒸饭的水汽浮浮。

一同商议祭祀之礼,点燃蒿草和牛脂。
取来公羊祭路神,烧之烤之,祈求下一个丰年。

我用木碗将祭品盛出,用木碗也用瓦器,香味开始升起。
上帝请您享受,这香味多么盛大。
自后稷开始受祀,从未有罪和悔,一直到如今。

  这首诗应该是祭祀后稷时的颂诗,回顾后稷神奇的一生,他不是肉体凡胎,出生时便展示了神迹。后来他擅长耕种,给予后人无限的恩泽。后人对他的祭祀,也非常有烟火气,舂米筛糠,淘米做饭,水汽浮动里,是人世间的幸福之感。此诗描述后稷的生平和功德,前半段是神话中的灵异色彩,后半段是现实中的烟火气息,两者交相辉映,共筑绚丽之景。

①攸介攸止:这里指等待胎儿长大成形。②震:通"娠",怀孕。③軷:祭祀路神。

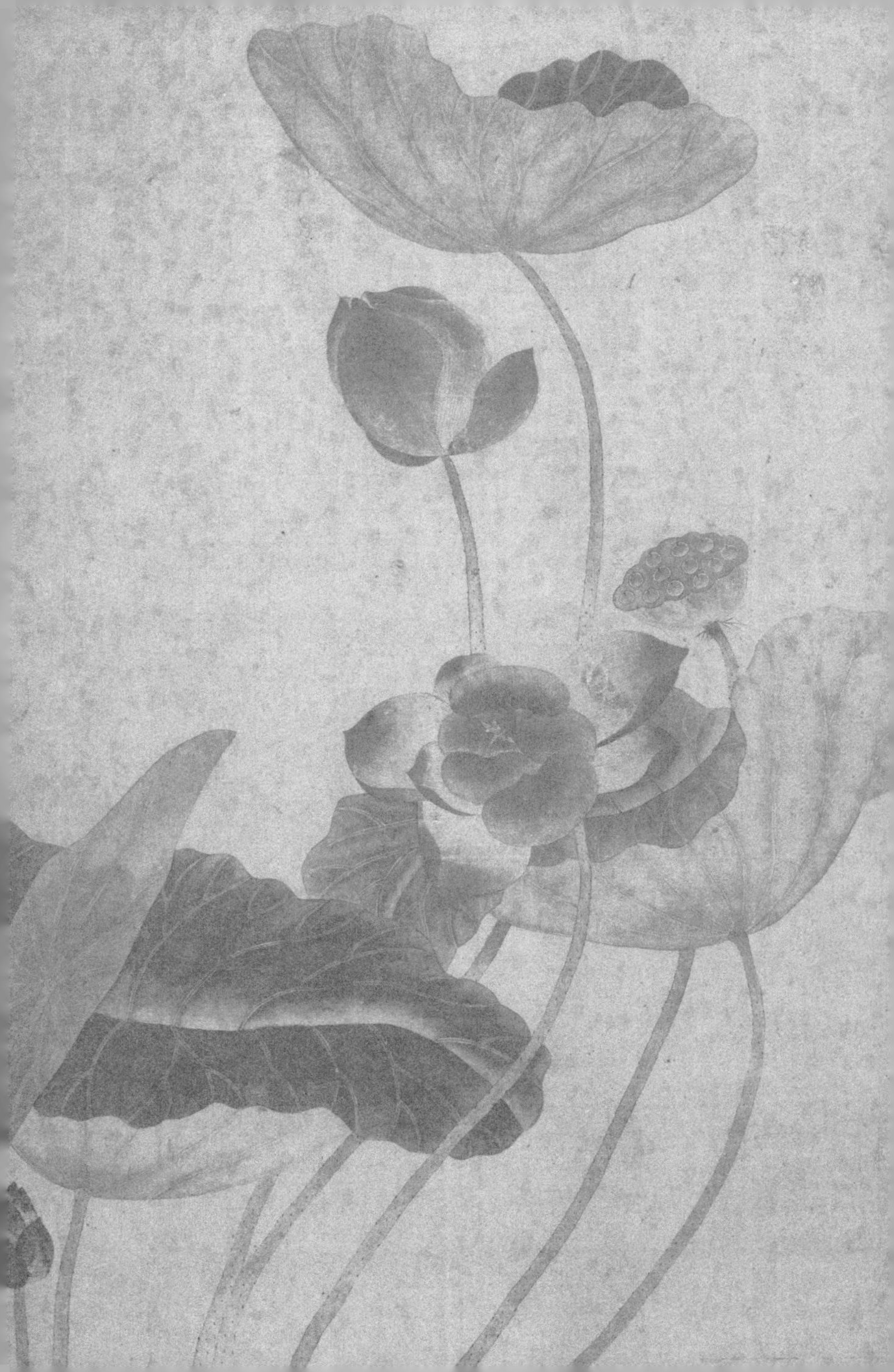

生民之什·行苇

敦彼行苇，牛羊勿践履。方苞方体，维叶泥泥。戚戚兄弟，莫远具尔。或肆之筵，或授之几。

肆筵设席，授几有缉御。或献或酢，洗爵奠斝。醓醢以荐，或燔或炙。嘉肴脾臄，或歌或咢。

敦弓既坚，四镞既钧，舍矢既均，序宾以贤。敦弓既句，既挟四镞。四镞如树，序宾以不侮。

曾孙维主，酒醴维醹，酌以大斗，以祈黄耇。黄耇台背，以引以翼。寿考维祺，以介景福。

Banquet

Let no cattle and sheep
Trample on roadside rush
Which bursts up with root deep
And with leaves soft and lush.
We're closely related brothers.
Let us be seated near.
Spread mats for some; for others
Stools will be given here.

Mats spread one on another,
Servants come down and up.
Host and guests pledge each other;
They rinse and fill their cup.
Sauce brought with prickles ripe
And roast or broiled meat,
There are provisions of tripe,
All sing to music sweet.

The bow prepared is strong
And the four arrows long.
The guests all try to hit
And stand in order fit.
They fully draw the bow
And four arrows straight go.
They hit like planting trees;
Those who miss stand at ease.

The grandson is the host;
With sweet or strong wine they toast.
They drink the cups they hold
And pray for all the old.
The hoary old may lead
And help the young in need.
May their old age be blessed;
May they enjoy their best!

芦苇丛丛生道边,牛羊不要踩踏。

刚刚打苞抽枝,你看那叶子柔润。

相亲相爱的兄弟,不要互相疏远。

宴席上谁在陈设竹案,谁去搬来木几。

摆好宴席,侍者接连端上去。

主客之间忙举杯,洗净杯盏敬酒频。

肉汁肉酱花样多,烧肉烤肉都呈上。

百叶牛舌皆味美,高歌击鼓心欢畅。

雕弓挽起强有力,四支利箭势如一。

所有箭矢皆中的,且以贤德排座席。

雕弓拉满如圆月,四支利箭俱在弦。

四支利箭树靶上,不以成败排座席。

曾孙乃是主人,拿出甜酒醇厚。

且用大杯斟满,祈祝老者年岁长。

老人年岁已高,还能引导晚辈。

长寿之人是人瑞,上天赐他好福气。

《乡土中国》里说，国人是以血缘为纽带，形成一个个团体。对于血亲的友善，历来被强调，像这首诗里，对于兄弟仁爱，以及对老人的善待，体现了国人传统的忠厚之风。看上去是一次追欢逐乐的宴席，但实质是家族的团建，彰显了家和万事兴的伦理道德。

生民之什·既醉

既醉以酒,既饱以德。君子万年,介尔景福。
既醉以酒,尔殽既将。君子万年,介尔昭明。
昭明有融,高朗令终。令终有俶,公尸嘉告。
其告维何?笾豆静嘉。朋友攸摄,摄以威仪。
威仪孔时,君子有孝子。孝子不匮,永锡尔类。
其类维何?室家之壸。君子万年,永锡祚胤。
其胤维何?天被尔禄。君子万年,景命有仆。
其仆维何?釐尔女士。釐尔女士,从以孙子。

Sacrificial Ode

We've drunk wine strong
And thank your grace.
May you live long!
Long live your race!

We've drunk wine strong
And eaten food.
May you live long!
Be wise and good!

Be good and wise!
By God you're led.
See spirit rise
And speak for our dead.

What does he say?
Your food is fine.
Constant friends stay
At the service divine.

With constant friends
And filial sons
There won't be end
For pious ones.

To you belong
The pious race.
May you live long!
Be blessed with grace!

Your race appears
By Heaven blessed.
You'll live long years,
Served east and west.

Who will serve you?
You will have maids and men.
Their sons will renew
Their service again.

您的美酒令我酩酊，您的美德令我丰足。
君子千秋万代，天赐您宏大的幸福。

您的美酒令我酩酊，您的佳肴频频端上。
君子千秋万代，天赐您永远道路光明。

道路光明又长远，您的嘉誉贯彻始终。
愿您总是善始善终，神灵良言且细听。

神灵要对您说什么？盛祭品的容器洁而美。
朋友们都来帮助，成就这隆重的祭礼。

这祭礼的礼节很合宜，君子总有孝子举祭。
孝子源源不尽，永远赐福给你的家族。

你的家族什么样？家中后嗣绵长。
君子千秋万代，上天赐你的子孙永享福禄。

你的子孙什么样？老天给予好福气。
君子千秋万代，命里无数人追随。

追随者都是啥样？赐你男男女女。
赐你男男女女，子子孙孙绵长。

此诗是西周时期的祖庙祭歌。祭祀临近尾声时，祝官感谢主人的招待，并且传递神灵的声音。享受祭祀的"祖先"也祝愿"君子"能够子孙无尽，让烟火一直传承下去。此诗结构匀称，形式完美，独具艺术特色。

①将：行。朱熹译为"持而进之"。②壸：宫中之巷，形容深而远。

生民之什·凫鹥

凫鹥在泾,公尸来燕来宁。尔酒既清,尔殽既馨。公尸燕饮,福禄来成。

凫鹥在沙,公尸来燕来宜。尔酒既多,尔殽既嘉。公尸燕饮,福禄来为。

凫鹥在渚,公尸来燕来处。尔酒既湑,尔殽伊脯。公尸燕饮,福禄来下。

凫鹥在潀,公尸来燕来宗,既燕于宗,福禄攸降。公尸燕饮,福禄来崇。

凫鹥在亹,公尸来止熏熏。旨酒欣欣,燔炙芬芬。公尸燕饮,无有后艰。

The Ancestor's Spirit

On the stream waterbirds appear;
On earth descends the Spirit good.
Your wine is sweet and clear,
And fragrant is your food.
The Spirit comes to drink and eat;
Your blessing will be sweet.

On the sand waterbirds appear;
On earth enjoys the Spirit good.
Abundant is your wine clear;
Delicious is your food.
The Spirit comes to drink and eat;
Your blessing will be complete.

On the isle waterbirds appear;
In his place sits the Spirit good.
Your wine is pure and clear;
In slices are your meat and food.
The Spirit eats and drinks sweet wine;
You will receive blessing divine.

Waterbirds swim where waters meet;
The Spirit sits in a high place.
In his high place he drinks wine sweet;
You will receive blessing and grace.
The Spirit drinks and eats his food;
You'll receive blessing doubly good.

In the gorge waterbirds appear;
Drunken on earth the Spirit good.
Delicious is your wine clear;
Broiled or roast your meat and food.
The Spirit comes to drink and feast;
You'll have no trouble in the least.

野鸭鸥鸟在泾水,先祖安然享受宴饮。

你的酒清醇,你的菜肴喷香,先祖宴饮,成就你的福禄。

野鸭鸥鸟在水边,先祖享受宴饮多么合宜。

你的酒繁多,你的菜肴美味。

先祖宴饮,帮你获得福禄。

野鸭鸥鸟在沙洲,先祖享受宴饮来你的居处。

你的酒多么澄澈,你的菜肴有肉脯。

先祖宴饮,福禄降临。

野鸭鸥鸟在港汊,先祖享受宴饮和尊敬。

宴席摆在宗庙里,福禄齐齐降临。

先祖宴饮,福禄重重。

野鸭鸥鸟在峡口,先祖赴宴多么和乐。

美酒令人醉醺醺,烧烤闻着香喷喷。

先祖宴饮,往后再无灾难。

这是周代贵族祭祀时演唱的赞美诗。有人扮演祖宗的神灵享受祭品，并且给予祭祀者各种祝福。祖宗享受得越多，祭祀者能够得到的福禄越多。"无有后艰"，是在赐福之外，又给上了一道保险；虽为祝词，却提出了预防灾害的问题，居安思危，也给予今人启发。

①尸：古代祭祀，代被祭者的神灵受祭的活人。②崇：重重。③公尸来止熏熏，旨酒欣欣：俞樾《古书疑义举例》里认为这句应该是"公尸来止欣欣，旨酒熏熏。"

生民之什·假乐

①假乐君子，显显令德，宜民宜人。受禄于天，保右命之，自天申之。

干禄百福，子孙千亿。穆穆皇皇，宜君宜王。不愆不忘，率由旧章。

威仪抑抑，德音秩秩。无怨无恶，率由群匹。受福无疆，四方之纲。

之纲之纪，燕及朋友③。百辟卿士，媚于天子。不解于位，民之攸塈。

King Cheng

Happy and good our king,
Of his virtue all sing.
He's good to people all;
On him all blessings fall
And favor from on high
Is renewed far and nigh.

They are blessed, everyone
Of his sons and grandsons.
He's majestic and great,
Fit ruler of the state.
Blameless and dutiful,
He follows father's rule.

His bearing dignified,
His virtue spreads far and wide.
From prejudice he's free,
Revered by all with glee.
He receives blessings great,
Modeled on from state to state.

He's modeled on without end;
Each state becomes his friend.
Ministers all and one
Admire the Heaven's Son.
Dutiful, he is blessed;
In him people find rest.

美好的周王，美德尽人皆知，能够安抚百姓，也善于使用大臣。

他受禄于天，老天保佑他也命令他，一再地申饬告诫他。

千禄百福，子孙千亿。

庄重又美好，适宜为君王。

没有过失不忘祖训，遵循旧规章。

仪表美好，政令清明。

无怨无恶，听从群臣。

受福无疆，四方都以他为纲。

他是世间纲纪，让公卿百官安然。

诸侯与群臣，皆爱此天子。

他忠于职守不懈怠，让人民能够休养生息。

老子说："太上，不知有之。"即好的统治者，老百姓不知道他的存在。这首诗里说"无怨无恶，率由群匹"，似乎周王没有自己的态度，一切都听大臣安排。但其实它是说周王的统治已经出神入化，能够让周围的人很自然地跟从他的领导，因为大家的利益是一致的。此诗中蕴含着对周王的深深赞美和殷切的希望。

①假乐：嘉乐。
②人：大臣。
③朋友：指朋友，也指诸臣。

文王曰咨，咨女殷商。天不湎尔以酒，不义从式。既愆尔止。靡明靡晦。式号式呼，俾昼作夜。

文王曰咨，咨女殷商。如蜩如螗，如沸如羹。小大近丧，人尚乎由行。内奰于中国，覃及鬼方。

文王曰咨，咨女殷商。匪上帝不时，殷不用旧。虽无老成人，尚有典刑。曾是莫听，大命以倾。

文王曰咨，咨女殷商。人亦有言：颠沛之揭，枝叶未有害，本实先拨。殷鉴不远，在夏后之世。

荡之什·荡

荡荡上帝,下民之辟。疾威上帝,其命多辟。天生烝民,其命匪谌。靡不有初,鲜克有终。

文王曰咨,咨女殷商。曾是强御?曾是掊克?曾是在位?曾是在服?天降滔德,女兴是力。

文王曰咨,咨女殷商。而秉义类,强御多怼。流言以对。寇攘式内。侯作侯祝,靡届靡究。

文王曰咨,咨女殷商。女炰烋于中国。敛怨以为德。不明尔德,时无背无侧。尔德不明,以无陪无卿。

Warnings

God's influence spreads vast
Over people below.
God's terror strikes so fast;
He deals them blow on blow.
Heaven gives people birth,
On whom he'd not depend.
At first they're good on earth,
But few last to the end.

"Alas!" said King Wen of the west,
"You king of Yin-Shang, lo!
How could you have oppressed
And exploited people so?
Why put those in high place
Who did everything wrong?
Why are those who love grace
Oppressed e'er by the strong?"

"Alas!" said King Wen of the west,
"You king of Yin-Shang, lo!
Why not help the oppressed
And give the strong a blow?
Why let rumors wide spread.
And robbers be your friend?
Let curse fall on your head
And troubles without end!"

"Alas!" said King Wen of the west,
"You king of Yin-Shang, lo!
You do wrong without rest.
Can good out of wrong grow?
You know not what is good;
You've no good men behind.
Good men not understood,
To you none will be kind."

"Alas!" said King Wen of the west,
"You king of Yin-Shang, lo!
You drink wine without rest;
On a wrong way you go.
You know not what's about,
Nor tell darkness from light.
Amid clamour and shout
You turn day into night."

"Alas!" said King Wen of the west,
"You king of Yin-Shang, lo!
Cicadas cry without rest
As bubbling waters flow.
Things great and small go wrong
But heedless still you stand.
Indignation grows strong
In and out of the land."

"Alas!" said King Wen of the west,
"You king Of Yin-Shang's days!
Not that you're not God-blessed,
Why don't you use old ways?
You've no experienced men,
But the laws have come down.
Why won't you listen then?
Your state will be o'erthrown."

* 238

"Alas!" said King Wen of the west,
"You who wear Yin-Shang's crown!
Know what say people blessed:
When a tree's fallen down,
Its leaves may still be green
But roots exposed to view.
Let Xia's downfall be seen
As a warning to you!"

    败坏法度的上帝，是下民之君。

    暴虐的上帝，他的命令多邪僻。

    老天生下这么多百姓，它的法令没有信用。

    开头还说得过去，但很少能够善终。

    文王说唉，唉你这殷商之主。

    竟然那么暴虐，竟然喜爱聚敛，竟然是在其位，竟然是在其职。

    老天降下无德之人，你却为他们助力。

    文王说唉，唉你这殷商之主。

    你仗着那些豪族，招来强敌之怨。

    你以流言去应对，让国内盗贼蜂起。

    大家彼此攻击诅咒，无休无止没完没了。

    文王说唉，唉你这殷商之主。

    你的咆哮回荡在这片大地上，招揽怨恨还以为是自己的功德。

你的德行之光已经熄灭,没有依靠也无人辅佐。

你的德行之光已经熄灭,没有人陪伴也无人爱戴。

文王说唉,唉你这殷商之主。

老天可没让你沉溺于酒,以不义为准则。

你是这样没有节制,没日没夜,大喊大叫,让白天变成黑夜。

文王说唉,唉你这殷商之主。

让这世界喧嚣如蝉鸣不已,混乱如沸羹。

让所有人行为都变得败坏,你只管一意孤行。

怒火在国内蔓延,乃至抵达远方。

文王说唉,唉你这殷商之主。

不是上帝不善良,殷商不用老规矩。

虽然没有老成之人,但还有典刑。

你完全不听,大命于是倾覆。

文王说唉,唉你这殷商之主。

人们曾经这么说:"大树倒伏树根撅起,树叶看似完好无损,但它的根本已经毁坏。"

殷的镜子其实没多远,就在夏桀那一代。

此诗借古讽今，警示周厉王接受殷王朝灭亡的历史教训，改弦更张。《毛诗序》："《荡》，召穆公伤周室大坏也。"说是周厉王无道，召穆公托文王之口，针砭商殷之弊，暗讽厉王。召穆公为了拯救周朝于将倾，也算煞费苦心。全诗构思巧妙，结构独特，具有较高的艺术价值。

①而秉义类：秉，用。义类，豪族。②炰烋：咆哮。③不明：不亮。

弓矢戎兵，用戒戎作，用遏蛮方。

③质尔人民，谨尔侯度，用戒不虞。慎尔出话，敬尔威仪，无不柔嘉。白圭之玷，尚可磨也；斯言之玷，不可为也！

无易由言，无曰『苟矣』，莫扪朕舌，言不可逝矣。无言不雠，无德不报。

惠于朋友，庶民小子。子孙绳绳，万民靡不承。

视尔友君子，辑柔尔颜，不遐有愆。相在尔室，尚不愧于屋漏。无曰不显，莫予云觏。神之格思，不可度思，④矧可射思！

⑤辟尔为德，俾臧俾嘉。淑慎尔止，不愆于仪。不僭不贼，鲜不为则。投我以桃，

荡之什·抑

①抑抑威仪,维德之隅。人亦有言:靡哲不愚,庶人之愚,亦职维疾。哲人之愚,亦维斯戾。

无竞维人,四方其训之。有觉德行,四国顺之。订谟定命,远犹辰告。敬慎威仪,维民之则。

其在于今,兴迷乱于政。颠覆厥德,荒湛于酒。女虽湛乐从,弗念厥绍。罔敷求先王,克共明刑。

肆皇天弗尚②,如彼泉流,无沦胥以亡。夙兴夜寐,洒扫庭内,维民之章。修尔车马,报之以李。彼童而角,实虹小子。

荏染柔木,言缗之丝。温温恭人,维德之基。其维哲人,告之话言,顺德之行。其维愚人,覆谓我僭。民各有心。

於乎小子,未知臧否。匪手携之,言示之事。匪面命之,言提其耳。借曰未知,亦既抱子。民之靡盈,谁夙知而莫成?

昊天孔昭,我生靡乐。视尔梦梦,我心惨惨。诲尔谆谆,听我藐藐。匪用为教,覆用为虐。借曰未知,亦聿既耄。

於乎小子,告尔旧止。听用我谋,庶无大悔。天方艰难,曰丧厥国。取譬不远,昊天不忒。回遹其德,俾民大棘。

Admonition by Duke Wu of Wei

What appears dignified
Reveals a good inside.
You know as people say:
There're no sages but stray.
When people have done wrong,
It shows their sight not long.
When sages make mistakes,
It shows their wisdom breaks.

If a leader is good,
He'll tame the neighborhood.
If his virtue is great,
He'll rule o'er every state,
When he gives orders,
They'll reach the borders.
As he is dignified,
He's obeyed far and wide.

Look at the present state:
Political chaos' great.
Subverted the virtue fine,
You are besotted by wine.
You wish your pleasure last
And think not of the past.
Enforce the laws laid down
By kings who wore a crown!

Or Heaven won't bless you
Like water lost to view,
Till you're ruined and dead.

Rise early, late to bed!
Try to sweep the floor clean;
Let your pattern be seen.
Keep cars and steeds in rows
And your arrows and bows.
If on alert you stand,
None dare invade your land.

Do people real good;
Make laws against falsehood.
Beware of what's unforeseen;
Say rightly what you mean.
Try to be dignified;
Be kind and mild outside.
A flaw in white jade found,
Away it may be ground;
A flaw in what you say
Will leave its influence to stay.

Don't lightly say a word
Nor think it won't be heard.
Your tongue is held by none;
Your uttered words will run.
Each word will answered be;
No deed is done for free.
If you do good to friend
And people without end,
You'll have sons in a string
And people will obey you as king.

* 245

Treat your friends with good grace;
Show them a kindly face.
You should do nothing wrong
E'en when far from the throng.
Be good when you're alone;
No wrong is done but known.
Think not you are unseen.
The sight of God is keen.
You know not what is in his mind,
Let alone what's behind.

When you do what is good,
Be worthy of manhood.
With people get along;
In manners do no wrong.
Making no mistakes small,
You'll be pattern for all.
For a peach thrown on you,
Return a plum as due.
Seeking horns where there's none,
You make a childish fun.

The soft, elastic wood
For stringed lute is good.
A mild, respectful man
Will do good when he can.
If you meet a man wise,
At what you say he tries
To do what he thinks good.
But a foolish man would.
Think what you say untrue:
Different is his view.

Alas! Young man, how could.
You tell evil from good?
I'll lead you by the hand.
And show you where you stand.
I'll teach you face to face.
So that you can keep pace.
I'll hold you by the ear,
You too have a son dear.
If you are not content,
In vain your youth is spent.

Great Heaven fair and bright,
I live without delight.
Seeing you dream all day,
My heart will pine away.
I tell you now and again,
But I advise you in vain.
You think me useless one;
Of my words you make fun.
Can you say you don't know
How old today you grow?

Alas! Young man, I pray,
Don't you know ancient way?
Listen to my advice,
And you'll be free from vice.
If Heaven's ire come down,
Our state would be o'erthrown.
Just take example near by,
You'll see justice on high.
If far astray you go,
You'll plunge people in woe.

礼仪严密，德行才能方正。

岂不闻人家说，不是聪明人就不会犯糊涂。

普通人愚蠢，那是天赋有缺陷。

聪明人犯糊涂，就会惹下大麻烦。

无可争锋要靠贤人，四方方能顺服。

你有大德行，四方能顺从。

大方针要作为法令坚定执行，大谋略要时常告知大众。

礼仪要恭敬谨慎，才能为百姓的榜样。

当今眼下，政事迷乱。

你的德行已颠覆，成天沉迷于酒。

你过度享乐，不念功业传承，不求先王之道，不能将法令执行。

皇天不会保佑你，你就像泉水随便淌，大家一起沉没吧。

本来你应该早起晚睡，洒扫庭内，为万民之榜样。

你应该修好你的车马，整理弓箭武器，准备战事忽起，征服远方的异族。

你应该安定你的人民，谨守君侯该守之法度，以防不测发生。

你应该谨慎发言，礼仪端庄，举手投足无不柔和美好。

你要知道白玉上有瑕疵，尚且可以磨除，说话有毛病，就没得救了。

说话不要太轻易，不要张嘴就说"随便"。
没有人会摁住我们的舌头，话说出来再无法追回。
没有哪句话会没有回应，没有哪种德行没有回报。
友善地对待群臣，以及庶民小子。
那样你的子孙无穷尽，万民无不顺服。

对待你的大臣贵族，要和颜悦色，自省何过之有。
在你家中，也仍要无愧于上天。
不要说："反正不明显，没有人能把我看清楚。"
神之所至，深不可测，何况还想猜中？

君之修德，使之高尚与美好。
善良谨慎，不要在礼仪上犯错。
不犯错也不凶残，很少不被别人拿去当榜样。
投我以桃，报之以李。
非说小羊头生角，实在是小子胡说八道。

柔韧之木，装上弦丝。
温和恭谨之人，是德行之根本。

如果你是聪明人，有人将箴言告诉你，你会按照美德行事。

如果你是糊涂人，反倒说我话有错，人心各异没法说。

唉，你这年轻人，不知好歹。
难道我没有将你拉扯，教你做事？
难道我没有当面指导你，还拎起你的耳朵？
假如说你不明事理，你也是当爹的人了。
人人都不完美，有谁是早晨就懂晚上能成。

苍天昭明，我这辈子不快乐。
看你像是在迷梦中，我心中更是惨淡。
我苦口婆心教导你，你吊儿郎当不听劝。
不把我的教导当回事，反而拿来开玩笑。
如果说你不懂事，其实你也老大不小。

唉，小子，让我告诉你先王的旧规矩。
你听我的主意，将来不会太后悔。
老天正让人世更加艰难，看来是要灭我们的国家。
参照物不用远求，老天做事没差池。
就这邪僻的德行，老百姓将有大急难。

此诗语言精练，警句频出，"夙兴夜寐""投桃报李"等成语都源于此诗。关于此诗的主旨，历来说法不一，比较主流的说法是卫武公自警兼刺平王，但看诗中字句，更像是老臣怒斥年少君主，老臣悲愤交加，少年君主则嘻嘻哈哈。这首诗虽然是单方面叙述，但画面感极强。

①抑抑：严密，周密。②尚：保佑。③质：安定。④矧可射思：矧，何况；射，猜度。⑤辟：君。

孔棘我圉。

为谋为毖,乱况斯削。告尔忧恤,诲尔序爵。谁能执热,逝不以濯?其何能淑,

载胥及溺。

如彼溯风,亦孔之僾。民有肃心,荓云不逮。好是稼穑,力民代食。稼穑维宝,

代食维好?

天降丧乱,灭我立王。降此蟊贼,稼穑卒痒。哀恫中国,具赘卒荒。靡有旅力,

以念穹苍。

维此惠君,民人所瞻。秉心宣犹,考慎其相。维彼不顺,自独俾臧。自有肺肠,

荡之什·桑柔

菀彼桑柔,其下侯旬,捋采其刘,瘼此下民。不殄心忧,仓兄填兮。倬彼昊天,宁不我矜?

四牡骙骙,旟旐有翩。乱生不夷,靡国不泯。民靡有黎,具祸以烬。於乎有哀,国步斯频。

国步蔑资,天不我将。靡所止疑,云徂何往?君子实维,秉心无竞。谁生厉阶,至今为梗?

忧心慇慇,念我土宇。我生不辰,逢天僤怒。自西徂东,靡所定处。多我觏痻,俾民卒狂。

瞻彼中林，牲牲其鹿。朋友已谮，不胥以谷。人亦有言：进退维谷。

维此圣人，瞻言百里。维彼愚人，覆狂以喜。匪言不能，胡斯畏忌？

维此良人，弗求弗迪。维彼忍心，是顾是复。民之贪乱，宁为荼毒。

大风有隧，有空大谷。维此良人，作为式谷。维彼不顺，征以中垢。

大风有隧，贪人败类。听言则对，诵言如醉。匪用其良，覆俾我悖。

嗟尔朋友，予岂不知而作。如彼飞虫，时亦弋获。既之阴女，反予来赫。

民之罔极，职凉善背③。为民不利，如云不克。民之回遹，职竞用力。

民之未戾，职盗为寇。凉曰不可，覆背善詈。虽曰匪予，既作尔歌！

Misery and Disorder

Lush are mulberry trees.
Their shade affords good ease.
When they're stript of their leaves,
The people deeply grieves.
They're so deeply distressed
That sorrow fills their breast.
O Heaven great and bright,
Why not pity our plight?

The steeds run far and nigh;
The falcon banners fly.
The disorder is great;
There's ruin in the state.
So many killed in clashes,
Houses reduced to ashes.
Alas! we're full of gloom;
The state is near its doom.

Nothing can change our fate;
Heaven won't help our state.
Where to stop sue don't know;
We have nowhere to go.
Good men may think and brood;
They strive not for their good.
Who is the man who sows.
The dire distress and woes?

With heavy heart I stand,
Thinking of my homeland.
Born at unlucky hour,
I meet God's angry power,
From the east to the west,
I have nowhere to rest.
I see only disorder;
In danger is our border.

If you follow advice,
You may lessen the vice.
Let's gain a livelihood;
Put things in order good.
Who can hold something hot.
If he waters it not?
Can remedy be found
If the people are drowned?

Standing against the breeze,
How can you breathe at ease?
Could people forward go
Should an adverse wind blow?
Love cultivated soil;
Let people live on toil.
The grain to them is dear;
They toil from year to year.

Heaven sends turmoil down
To ruin the royal crown.
Injurious insects reign
And devour crop and grain.
Alas! In Central State
Devastation is great.
What can I do but cry
To the boundless great sky?

If the king's good and wise,
He's revered in our eyes.
He'll make his plans with care
And choose ministers fair and square.
If he has no kinghood,
He'll think alone he's good.
His thoughts are hard to guess,
His people in distress.

Behold! Among the trees
The deer may roam at ease.
Among friends insincere
You cannot roam with cheer,
Nor advance nor retreat
As in a strait you meet.

How wise these sages are!
Their views and words reach far.
How foolish those men bad!
They rejoice as if mad.
We can't tell them what we know
For fear of coming woe.

These good men you avoid,
They are never employed.
Those cruel men in power.
Are courted from hour to hour.
So disorder is bred
And evil deeds wide spread.

The big wind blows a gale
From the large, empty vale.
What can a good man say?
It is of no avail!
In the court bad men stay;
What they say will prevail.

The big wind blows its way;
In the court bad men stay.
When praised, they're overjoyed;
When blamed, they play the drunk.
Good men are not employed;
In distress they are sunk.

Alas! Alas! My friend,
Can I write to no end?
Like a bird on the wing,
Hit, you may be brought down.
Good to you I will bring,
But at me you will frown.

Don't do wrong to excess;
People fall in distress.
If you do people wrong,
How can they get along?
If they take a wrong course,
It's because you use force.

People live in unrest,
For robbers spread like pest.
I say that will not do;
You say that is not true.
Though you think I am wrong,
I've made for you this song.

桑树嫩叶繁密,树下大片阴凉。
是谁将掉剩残枝,下方百姓遭殃。
我心忧思不绝,悲伤久久不去。
苍天如此广阔,为何不肯顾我?

看那驷马强壮,鹰蛇旗帜飘扬。
人间祸乱不息,诸国有谁安宁。
民间已无壮男,战火焚为灰烬。
叹声呜呼哀哉,国运就此危急。

国运艰难没钱,老天不肯助我。
哪里才能安居?不知该往哪去。
君子不妨想想,有无怀抱私心?
是谁制造祸端?至今仍是阻碍。

我自忧心忡忡,想念国土家园。
我自生不逢时,赶上老天发怒。
从西向东奔逃,没有地方安居。
我遭太多灾难,国家边疆危急。

谋划若是谨慎,祸患就会削减。
劝你忧恤天下,教你以贤择人。
谁能顶着炎热,不赶紧去洗濯?
事情做得不好,大家全都完蛋。

就像逆风而行,总是艰于呼吸。
民有进取之心,你使他力有不逮。
稼穑本是好事,百姓干活养你。
稼穑是件好事,你正好不劳而获。

老天降下丧乱,灭我所立之王。
降下这些害虫,让我庄稼遭殃。
哀哉我的中国,苍茫大地皆荒。
可叹回天无力,如何打动上苍。

像那贤德之君,百姓尽皆仰望。
他的心意如光明大道,谨慎选择卿相。
而那荒唐之君,只管自己安好。
自有一副肺肠,让老百姓发狂。

看那树林之中,鹿儿成群结队。
朋友彼此欺骗,不能友好相待。
你可曾有听说,若此进退两难。

看那聪明之人,一望百里之外。
看那愚蠢之人,反为眼下欢喜。
你非不能开口,为何顾忌重重?

看那善良之人,无求无所钻营。
看那残忍之人,贪婪无止无休。
百姓陷入贪乱,宁可为此荼毒。

大风有其来路，来自空空山谷。
那些善良之人，举止可为典范。
那些扭曲之人，总行龌龊之事。

大风有其来路，贪人就是败类。
人相劝就说对，背诵道理如醉。
不听忠良之言，反使我遭逆悖。

哎呀我的朋友，我岂不知你作为。
就像翩飞之鸟，有时也被擒获。
我早知你底细，反而将我吓唬。

百姓也没个准，只相信背信弃义之人。
你对百姓不利，还怕不能干成？
百姓要走歪路，你们推波助澜。

民心无法安定，执政者为盗贼。
劝你这样不可，反在背后骂我。
虽然将我非议，我也要为你写这首歌。

此诗是《诗经》中少有的大诗之一，全诗义正词严，典型地描述了一个政权行将崩溃时的种种迹象，诗人的忧患让人至为感动。周厉王残酷无道，老百姓为了求生，也不能够按照规矩来，天下丧乱；作为卿士的芮良夫左支右绌，愤怒不已。《诗序》里说，这首诗是"芮伯刺厉王也"，芮伯的激切从词句里一望而知。

此诗既叹百姓的穷困，又伤国事的昏乱；既探祸乱之根，又言救乱之道；既叹生不逢时，又伤救世无力；既指斥国君昏庸无能，又斥群僚不直言进谏；既斥责小人霍乱国家，又指斥君主用人不当，全诗充斥着沉郁和忧伤的家国情怀。

---

①代食：指不劳动的官僚坐吃粮食。②宣犹：宣，光明。犹，道路。③职凉善背：职，只。凉，相信。背，背信弃义。只相信背信弃义之人。

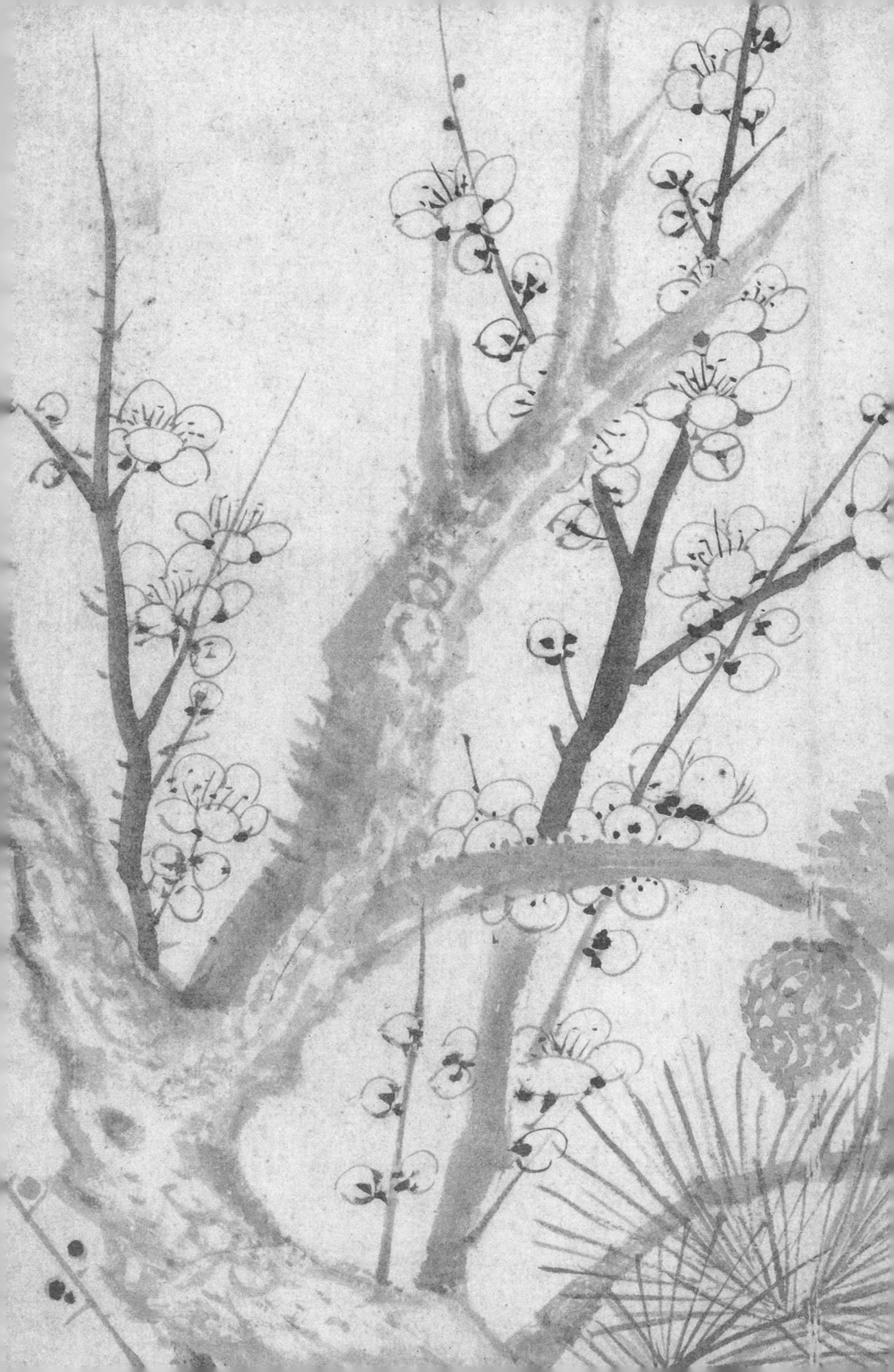

则不我助。父母先祖,胡宁忍予?

旱既大甚,涤涤山川。旱魃为虐,如惔如焚。我心惮暑,忧心如熏。群公先正,则不我闻。昊天上帝,宁俾我遯? ①dùn

旱既大甚,黾勉畏去。胡宁瘨我以旱?憯不知其故。祈年孔夙,方社不莫。昊天上帝,则不我虞。敬恭明神,宜无悔怒。

旱既大甚,散无友纪。鞫哉庶正,疚哉冢宰。趣马师氏,膳夫左右。靡人不周,无不能止。瞻卬昊天,云如何里!

旱既大甚,黾勉畏去。瞻卬昊天,有嘒其星。大夫君子,昭假无赢。大命近止,无弃尔成。何求为我,以戾庶正。瞻卬昊天,曷惠其宁?

荡之什·云汉

倬彼云汉,昭回于天。王曰:於乎!何辜今之人?天降丧乱,饥馑荐臻。靡神不举,靡爱斯牲。圭璧既卒,宁莫我听?

旱既大甚,蕴隆虫虫。不殄禋祀,自郊徂宫。上下奠瘗,靡神不宗。后稷不克,上帝不临。耗斁下土,宁丁我躬。

旱既大甚,则不可推。兢兢业业,如霆如雷。周余黎民,靡有孑遗。昊天上帝,则不我遗。胡不相畏?先祖于摧。

旱既大甚,则不可沮。赫赫炎炎,云我无所。大命近止,靡瞻靡顾。群公先正,

Great Drought

The Silver River shines on high,
Revolving in the sky.
The king heaves sigh on sigh:
"O what wrong have we done?
What riot has death run!
Why have famines come one by one?
What sacrifice have we not made?
We have burned all maces of jade.
Have we not killed victims in herd?
How is it that we are not heard?

"The drought has gone to excess;
The heat has caused distress.
There's no sacrifice we've not made;
For gods above we've buried jade.
There are no souls we don't revere
In temples far and near.
The Lord of Corn can't stop the drought;
Ruin falls on on our land all about.
The Almighty God won't come down.
Why should the drought fall on my crown!

"Excessive is the drought;
I am to blame, no doubt.
I palpitate With fear.
As if thunder I hear.
Of people I'm bereft;
How many will be left?
The Almighty on high
Does not care if we die.
O my ancestors dear,
Don't you extinction fear?

"Excessive is the drought;
No one can put it out.
The sun burns far and wide;
I have nowhere to hide.
Our end is coming near;
I see no help appear.
Dukes and ministers dead
All turn away the head.
O my ancestors dear,
How can you not appear?

"The drought spreads far and nigh;
Hills are parched and streams dry.
The demon vents his ire;
He spreads wide flame and fire.
My heart's afraid of heat;
Burned with grief, it can't beat.
Why don't the souls appear?
Won't they my prayer hear?
Almighty in the sky,
Why put on me such pressure high?

"The drought holds excessive sway,
But I dare not go away.
Why has it come from on high?
I know not the reason why.
Early I prayed for a good year,
Sacrifice offered there and here.
God in heaven, be kind!

Why won't you bear this in mind?
O my reverend sire,
Why vent on me your ire?

"The drought has spread far and near;
People dispersed there and here.
Officials toil in vain;
The premier brings no rain.
The master of my horses
And leaders of my forces,
There's none but does his best;
There's none who takes a rest.
I look up to the sky.
What to do with soil dry?

"I look up to the sky;
The stars shine bright on high.
My officers have done their best;
With rain our land's not blessed.
Our course of life is run,
But don't give up what's done.
Pray for rain not for me
But for officials on the knee.
I look up to the sky:
Will rain and rest come from on high?"

银河苍茫浩瀚，星斗明亮，旋转于天。

国王一声长叹，说当今之人何辜？老天降此丧乱，饥馑接二连三。

有哪位神我们不曾祭祀，何尝吝惜祭祀的牺牲。

圭璧都已用尽，为什么我们的声音没有人听？

这旱灾无边无际，天地如蒸笼，热气腾腾。

不断地祭祀，从郊外到庙中。

从天神到地神，没有哪个神我们不恭敬。

后稷不肯保佑我们，上天不肯降下恩德。

下方的土地尽遭损害,苦难落在我身上。

这旱灾无边无际,完全无法消除。
我们兢兢业业,上天如雷如霆。
周地所余黎民,没有剩下几个。
苍天啊大地啊,不肯对我施恩。
为什么你们不害怕呢?子孙断绝,还有谁来祭祀?

这旱灾无边无际,完全无法止住。
烈日赫赫炎炎,我没有容身之地。
我的生命就要终结。有谁将我看顾?
天上的公卿诸侯,不肯将我帮助。
父母啊先祖啊,你们怎么忍心看我受苦?

这旱灾无边无际,荡尽山川河流。
旱魔何其肆虐,像大火要焚尽一切。
我心中害怕酷暑,忧心若烟火熏烤。
天上的公卿诸侯,不听我的声音。
苍天啊大地啊,你让我怎么逃?

这旱灾无边无际,我勤勉地祈祷不敢离去。
为什么用旱灾折磨我?我一直不知道缘故。
祈年祭祀很早,祭四方神和灶神不晚。
苍天啊大地啊,却不肯将我帮助。

我敬恭神明，应该不会对我恼怒。

这旱灾无边无际，世间散乱没有法纪。
百官陷入困窘，宰相无比焦虑。
马官与教官，膳夫和左右大臣。
没有人不帮忙，但都不能终结。
仰望苍天，我何其忧伤。
仰望苍天，星光明亮。

大夫君子，祈祷上天多么虔诚。
我的生命就要终结，不要放弃你们的努力。
哪里是为我而求，是为了安定诸卿。
仰望苍天，何时能赐予天下安宁。

  这是周宣王祈雨时的诗作。开头两句写星河浩瀚，流光溢彩，更显出苍天无情。周宣王扪心自问，每个神灵面前他都祈求，每一场祭祀他都不敢掉以轻心，他后来不得不使出撒手锏，问上天先祖：如果百姓死绝了，还有谁来给他们祭祀？

  旱灾让世间失序，令百官陷入焦虑。周宣王仰望苍穹，一再发出绝望之声。虽然君主的祈祷更多的是一种仪式，但这首诗写得情真意切，将读者带入他的焦虑里，产生极强的艺术感染力。

①遯：通"遁"，逃。

钩膺濯濯。

王遣申伯，路车乘马。我图尔居，莫如南土。锡尔介圭，以作尔宝。往近王舅，

南土是保。

申伯信迈，王饯于郿。申伯还南，谢于诚归。王命召伯，彻申伯土疆。以峙其粻，

式遄其行。

申伯番番，既入于谢。徒御啴啴。周邦咸喜，戎有良翰。不显申伯，王之元舅，

文武是宪。

申伯之德，柔惠且直。揉此万邦，闻于四国。吉甫作诵，其诗孔硕。其风肆好，

以赠申伯。

荡之什·崧高

崧高维岳,骏极于天。维岳降神,生甫及申。维申及甫,维周之翰。四国于蕃,四方于宣。

①亹亹申伯,王缵②之事。于邑于谢,南国是式。王命召伯,定申伯之宅。③登是南邦,世执其功。

王命申伯,式是南邦。因是谢人,以作尔庸。王命召伯,彻申伯土田。王命傅御,迁其私人。

申伯之功,召伯是营。有俶其城,寝庙既成。既成藐藐,王锡申伯。四牡蹻蹻,

Count of Shen

The four mountains ate high;
Their summits touch the sky.
Their spirits come on earth
To Fu and Shen gave birth.
The Shen State and Fu State
Are Zhou House's bulwarks great.
They screen it from attack
On the front and the back.

Count Shen was diligent
In royal government.
At Xie he set up capital,
A pattern for southern states all.
Count Shao Was ordered by the king.
To take charge of the house-building.
Of southern states Shen's made the head,
Where his great influence will spread.

The king ordered Shen's chief
To be pattern to southern fief,
And employ men of capital
To build the city wall.
The king gave Count Shao his command
To define Count Shen's land.
The king ordered his steward old
To remove Shen's household.

The construction of State of Shen.
Was done by Count Shao and his men.
They built first city walls
And then the temple halls,
The great works done by the lord,
The king gave Count Shen as reward
Four noble steeds at left and right
With breasthooks amid trappings bright.

The king told Count Shen to speed
To his State in cab and steed.
"I've thought of your town beforehand;
Nowhere's better than southern land.
I confer on you this mace,
Symbol of dignity and grace.
Go, my dear uncle, go
And protect the south from the foe."

Count Shen set out for Xie;
The king feasted him at Mei.
Count Shen would take command
At Xie in southern land.
Count Shao was ordered to define.
Shen's land and border line,
And provide him with food
That he might find his journey good.

Count Shen with flags and banners
Came to Xie, grand in manners.
His footmen and charioteers
Were greeted by the town with cheers.
The state will be guarded by men
Under the command of Count Shen,
Royal uncle people adore
And pattern in peace as in war.

Count Shen with virtue bright
Is mild, kind and upright.
He'll keep all states in order,
With fame spread to the border.
I, Ji Fu, make this song.
In praise of the count strong
I present this beautiful air.
To the count bright ad fair.

山岭高大莫过四岳,高耸直插入天空。
四月降下神灵,生出甫侯与申伯。
那个甫侯与申伯,是这周朝的栋梁。
四国以他为藩篱,四方以他为垣墙。

勤勉的申伯,继承辅佐王室之事。
建立城邑在谢地,成为南国典范。
周王命令召伯,确定申伯的宅地。
建成南方的城邑,世代守着这功绩。

周王命令申伯,建成南方的榜样。
依靠这些谢人,建成你的城池。

周王命令召伯,确定申伯的土田。
周王命令大臣,帮申伯搬迁家臣。

申伯创立功业,召伯帮他经营。
于是始建城池,寝庙一同建成。
建成这深宅大院,国王赐予申伯。
骏马四匹肥硕,钩环缨带晶莹。

周王派遣申伯,乘坐驷马高车:
"我想你的居处,唯有南邦最好。赐你诸侯封圭,作为宝物收藏。去吧王舅,护佑我的南土。"

申伯再住一晚,周王饯行于郿。
申伯回到南方,诚心定居谢邑。
周王命令召伯,确定申伯土疆。
准备足够的粮食,使申伯快回南方。

申伯姿态昂扬,回到谢邑南方,步兵和骑手众多。
四方欢喜不胜,你们有了栋梁。
赫赫申伯,周王的大舅,文武的榜样。

申伯之德,柔惠又正直。
治理此万邦,美誉传四方。
吉甫写下这首诗,这首诗很长。
它词意深长,愿为申伯增光。

《诗序》说,此诗为"尹吉甫美宣王也",周宣王增加舅舅申伯的封地,还派召伯帮他建立城池,划定疆域,说起来本是他家的私事,但在当时体现了周宣王"能建国亲诸侯",不将权力完全握在自己手中的高风亮节。其实,周宣王分封申伯于谢是有其政治目的,完全是以巩固周王室的统治为出发点的。

①亹亹:勤勉。②缵:继承。③登:成。④徒御啴啴:徒,步兵。御,骑兵。啴啴,众多。

维天之命

第五章

CHAPTER FIVE

Great Heaven goes its way

清庙之什·清庙

於穆清庙,肃雍显相。
济济多士,秉文之德。
对①越在天,骏奔走在庙②。
不显③不承,无射于人斯。

King Wen's Temple

Solemn's the temple still;
Princes their duties fulfil.
Numerous officers,
Virtuous King Wen's followers.
Worship his soul on high,
Whom they hurry to glorify.
There are none but revere
Tirelessly their ancestor dear.

噫，庙宇幽深宁静，显赫的助祭者庄重雍容。

执事之人济济一堂，秉承着文王之德。

面对天上神灵，疾奔于庙中。

文王之德被凸显，被尊奉，不弃于人间。

    此诗通常认为是周王祭祖时所作的乐歌，对于庙宇和祭祀场面的描述，烘托出庄严的气氛。此诗通过对告祭致政祀典的礼赞，表达了对周人祖先功德的感谢和企盼德业永继的愿望，强化了周人天命王权的神圣理念。

①越：于。②骏：迅速。③不：助词。

清庙之什·维天之命

维天之命,①於穆不已。
於乎不显,文王之德之纯。
②假以溢我,③我其收之。
骏④惠我文王,曾孙笃之。

King Wen Deified

Great Heaven goes its way
Without cease and for aye.
O King Wen's virtue great
Will likewise circulate.
His virtue overflows
 And in his descendants grows.
Whatever King Wen has done
Will profit his grandson.

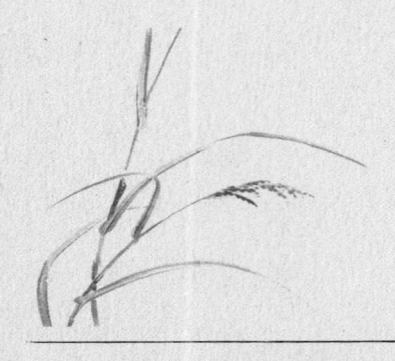

天道,

啊,肃穆无边。

啊,多么光明,文王之德纯净。

仁政漫溢到我身上,我收之。

我顺承文王之德,子孙也很忠诚。

这首祭祀的乐歌认为,文王的美德会惠及无穷远。此诗言辞古直,情意朴素,虽篇幅不长,但充满了恭敬之意、颂扬之辞。

①於:叹词。②假:好处,益处。③溢:漫溢。④惠:顺从。

清庙之什·维清

维清缉熙，文王之典。肇禋①，迄用有成，维周之祯②。

King Wen's Statutes

The world is clear and bright;
King Wen's statutes shed light.
Begin by sacrificial rite
And end by victory great.
God, bless Zhou's State!

唯有清澈光明才是值得延续的光明,就像文王之典。

开始祭祀,直到有所成就,是周家的吉祥。

这首诗将文王法典提到前所未有的高度,认为这个法典带给周家吉祥。这在强调君权天命的年代十分罕见。也有后人认为,此诗是歌颂文王武功的祭祀乐舞的歌辞。

①缉熙:光熙,明。②祯:吉祥。

清庙之什·烈文

烈文辟公①,锡兹祉福。惠我无疆,子孙保之。无封靡于尔邦②,维王其崇之。念兹戎功,继序其皇之。无竞维人,四方其训之③。不显维德,百辟其刑之④。於乎,前王不忘!

King Cheng's Inaugural Address

O princes bright and brave
Favored by former kings!
Boundless blessings we have
Will pass to our of springs.
Don't sin against your state
And you'll be honored as before.

Think of your service great
You may enlarge still more.
Try to employ wise men,
Your influence will spread from land to land.
Try to practise virtue then
Your good example will forever stand.
O of all things,
Forget not former kings!

有功德的各位诸侯,上天赐此福祉。

给我们恩惠无疆,子孙要保住这一切。

不要在你的国家犯下大错,要尊崇文王之德。

念着这些大功劳,继承并且发扬光大。

要想没有对手,得有人才,四方都会顺从。

想要显耀得靠道德,诸侯都会效仿。

哎呀,不要忘掉前王。

  周成王祭祖,诸侯助祭,这首乐歌既有训诫,也有劝勉。此诗虽没有点出"君臣"二字,但其含义却更加深刻:诸侯功绩再大,也不过是尽臣子的本分;周王的号令诸侯,才是行君临天下的威仪,并将延绵至子孙万代。

①辟公:诸侯。②封靡:大罪。③训:顺服。④刑:仿效。

清庙之什·天作

天作高山,大王荒之。彼作矣,文王康之。彼徂矣,岐有夷之行①。子孙保之。

Mount Qi

Heaven made lofty hill
For former kings to till.
King Tai worked the land
For King Wen to expand.
The former kings are gone;
The mountain path is good to travel on.
O ye son and grandson,
Pursue what your forefathers have begun!

老天生此高山,太王前来开荒。

百姓在这里经营,文王带他们享受安康。

他们来到这里,岐山有了平坦大道,子孙将其守护。

此诗讲述太王和文王开疆拓土的功绩,叮嘱后世铭记莫忘。此诗也是祭祀太王的乐歌,将圣地、圣人的歌颂融为一体,着力描写积蓄力量的进程,揭示历史发展的必然趋势。此诗语言质朴无华,文笔如瀑布飞流直泻;短短七句,有如此艺术效果,可见作者的大手笔。

①夷:平坦。

臣工之什·臣工

嗟嗟臣工,敬尔在公。王厘尔成,来咨来茹。
嗟嗟保介,维莫之春,亦又何求?如何新畬?
於皇来牟,将受厥明。明昭上帝,迄用康年。
命我众人:②庤乃③钱镈,奄观④铚艾。

Husbandry

Ah! Ye ministers dear,
Attend to duties here.
The king's set down the rule,
You Should know to the full.
Ah! Ye officers dear,
It is now late spring here.
What do you seek to do?
Tend the fields old and new.

Wheat grows lush in the field.
What an enormous yield!
Ah! Heaven bright and clear
Will give us a good year.
Men, get ready to wield
Your sickles, spuds and hoes
And reap harvest in rows.

嗟嗟,你们这些臣工。

要虔敬地对待你们的公事。

君王赐给你们成就,你们要经常来谋划来商议。

嗟嗟,你们这些农官,在这暮春时节,有什么要求?

如何耕种已经开垦三年的熟田?

啊,这美好的大麦小麦,即将长成。

英明的上帝,给我以丰年。命令我等众人:准备好农具,尤其是快点查看你的镰刀。

这是周王耕种籍田并劝诫农官的农事诗。周王在春天到来之际,告诫大臣与农官要认真对待农事,同时祈愿苍天风调雨顺,给自己以丰年。

①厘:赐。②庤:储放。③钱镈:农具的名称。④铚艾:镰刀。

臣工之什·噫嘻

噫嘻成王,既昭假尔。
率时农夫,播厥百谷。
骏发尔私①,终三十里。
亦服尔耕,十千维耦②。

King Kang's Prayer

O King Cheng in the sky,
Please come down from on high.
See us lead the campaign
To sow all kinds of grain,
And till our fields with glee
All over thirty li!
Ten thousand men in pairs
Plough the land with the shares.

噫嘻成王，曾经召请你们到来。

率领着农夫，播种百谷。

抓紧开垦这些私田，三十里外是尽头。

都来耕种你们的田地，人山人海并肩耕地。

朱熹认为此诗是周成王劝诫农官之作。其具体地反映周初的农业生产和典礼实况，具有较高的史料价值和文学价值。

①私：私田。②耦：两人各持一耜并肩而耕。

臣工之什·振鹭

振鹭于飞,于彼西雍。我客戾止,亦有斯容。
在彼无恶,在此无斁。庶几夙夜,以永终誉。

The Guest Assisting at Sacrifice

Rows of egrets in flight
Over the marsh in the west.
Like those birds dressed in white,
Here comes our noble guest.
He's loved in his own State;
He is welcome in ours.
Be it early or late,
His fame for ever towers.

鹭鸟群飞,在那西边水泽上。
我的客人光临,也有着鹭鸟般优雅的仪容。
他在彼处无恶缘,在此处无人厌憎。
望您日夜多勤勉,总伴随美好名声。

通常认为这首诗是说周天子祭祀时,夏商后人来助祭。然而,看文辞,似乎又像是赞美被祭祀之人;此处与彼处,也许指的是灵界与人间。此诗比拟生动,情意殷切,内容丰沛。

臣工之什·丰年

丰年多黍多稌，亦有高廪，万亿及秭。为酒为醴，烝畀祖妣。以洽百礼，降福孔皆。

Thanksgiving

Millet and rice abound this year;
High granaries stand far and near.
There are millions of measures fine;
We make from them spirits and wine
And offer them to ancestors dear.
Then we perform all kinds of rite
And call down blessings from. Heaven bright.

丰年小米大米皆有余，粮仓高耸，亿万计量。

做成清酒与甜酒，献给祖宗。

以汇合百种礼物，请福分普遍降临。

这是周人庆丰年祭田神的乐诗。在秋冬祭礼上，将丰收之喜悦反映给祖先，向其祈福，并祈求神灵保佑。

臣工之什·有瞽

有瞽有瞽,在周之庭。设业设虡(jù),崇牙树羽。
①应田县鼓,②鞉③磬柷圉。既备乃奏,箫管备举。
喤喤厥声,肃雍和鸣,先祖是听。我客戾止,
永观厥成。

Temple Music

Musicians blind, musicians blind,
Come to the temple court behind.
The plume-adorned posts stand
With teeth-like frames used by the band;
From them suspend drums large and small,
And sounding stones withal.
Music is played when all's complete;
We hear pan-pipe, flute and drumbeat.
What sacred melody
And solemn harmony!
Dear ancestors, give ear;
Dear visitors, come here!
You will enjoy our song
And wish it to last long.

盲乐师啊盲乐师，在周朝宗庙的大庭。

摆下钟架鼓架，架子上彩羽飘拂。

有大鼓有小鼓有挂着的鼓，有摇鼓也要磬石枳和圉。

准备好了就演奏，箫管齐备。

声音洪亮和谐，和声肃穆庄严，祖先请您倾听。

我的客人到此，长久地注视着，直到一曲终了。

此诗是描写作乐的篇章，反映了周朝礼乐并重的传统观念。祭礼上的音乐，乐器琳琅满目，声音洪亮而和谐。此诗不仅体现出周朝音乐成就的辉煌，而且对周人"乐由天作"做了新的诠释。

①应田县：应，小鼓。田，大鼓。县，悬挂的鼓。②鞉：摇鼓。③枳圉：分别用在开始与结束时的两种乐器。

* 295

臣工之什·潜

猗与漆沮,潜有多鱼。有鳣有鲔,鲦鲿鰋鲤。以享以祀,以介景福。

Sacrifice of Fish

In Rivers Ju and Qi
Fish in warrens we see.
There're sturgeons large and small,
Mudfish, carp we enthral
For temple sacrifice
That we may be blessed twice.

啊,漆水与沮水,深处柴堆里有很多鱼。

有鳣有鲔,鲦鲿鰋鲤。

做成祭品祭祖宗,用以祈福向神灵。

将柴堆置于水里,拦截鱼儿,这是一种捕鱼方式。那么多种鱼作为祭品,也符合《丰年》说的"以洽百礼"。此诗篇幅虽短,但却罗列了六种鱼名和两处水域,可谓匠心独运,形象生动,意趣盎然。

闵予小子之什·闵予小子

闵予小子,遭家不造,嬛嬛在疚。於乎皇考,永世克孝。念兹皇祖,陟降庭止。维予小子,夙夜敬止。于乎皇王,继序思不忘。

Elegy on King Wu

Alas! How sad am I!
Over my deceased father I cry.
Lonely, I'm in distress
To lose my father whom gods bless.
Filial all your life long,
You loved grandfather strong
As if he were ever in courtyard.
Fatherless, I am thinking hard
Of you both night and day.
O kings to be remembered for aye!

可怜我这小子,家中遭遇不幸,令我孤独伤心。

唉我的父亲,永世都能坚持孝道。

想起我的先祖,请你们时常降保王。

我这小子,白天黑夜处事恭谨。

哎我的先王,我继承伟业永志不忘。

　　此诗是周成王将要执政时,朝拜于祖庙,祭告其父王周武王和祖父周文王的诗。成王祭祀文王武王,自称孤独的小子,旨在向祖先神灵祷告,祈求先祖光临庙庭,保佑周朝基业永续。

①不造:不幸。②嬛嬛:孤独。

闵予小子之什·访落

访予落止，率时昭考①。於乎悠哉，朕未有艾。
将予就之，继犹判涣②。维予小子，未堪家多难。
绍庭上下③，陟降厥家。休矣皇考④，以保明其身。

King Cheng's Ascension to The Throne

I take counsel on early days:
How to follow my father's ways?
Ah! But he is far above me
And to reach him I am not free.
Please help me to get to his side,
To learn on what I should decide.
I am a young king not so great.
To shoulder hard tasks of the state.
I will follow him up and down,
Take counsel to secure the crown.
Rest in peace, royal father dear,
O help me to be bright and clear!

在我继位之初，便追随父王之德。

哎呀，那是多么远大，我如何跟得上他。

我努力追随，依然精力分散。

我这小子啊，不能承受家中多难。

继承公正从上到下，提拔和贬谪那些大臣。

父皇请您安好啊，以保佑我身。

周成王祭祀周武王的谦虚之词。此诗既是周王室决心巩固政权的宣言，也是对武王之灵的宣誓，又是对诸侯的政策交代。

①昭考：指周武王。②涣：分散。③绍庭：绍，继承。庭，公正。④休：安。

闵予小子之什·敬之

敬之敬之,天维显思,命不易哉。无日高高在上,
陟降厥士,日监在兹。
维予小子,不聪敬止。日就月将,学有缉熙于光明。^①佛时仔肩,示我显德行。

King Cheng's Consultation

"Be reverent, be reverent!
The Heaven's way is evident.
Do not let its favor pass by
Nor say Heaven's remote on high.
It rules over our rise and fall
And daily watches over all."

"I am a young king of our state,
But I will show reverence great.
As sun and moon shine day and night,
I will learn to be fair and bright.
Assist me to fulfill my duty
And show me high virtue and beauty!"

警惕谦恭，天道高明，天命不容易保有。

不要说它高高在上，它随时升降关注万事，每天查看这块土地。

我这小子啊，不聪明也不够谨慎。

日积月累，学着让光明逐渐累积。

担当责任，请示我以光明的德行。

朱熹认为此诗前半部分是群臣劝诫成王，后半部分是成王诫勉自己。成王自谓性既不聪，行又不敬，但愿奋发学习，日积月累，便可达到光明的境界。

①佛：通"弼"，辅助。

闵予小子之什·小毖

予其惩,而毖后患。莫予荓蜂,自求辛螫。
肇允彼桃虫,拚飞维鸟。未堪家多难,予又集于蓼。

King Cheng's Self-criticism

I blame myself for woes gone by
And guard against those of future nigh.
A wasp is a dangerous thing.
Why should I seek its painful sting?
At first only a wren is heard;
When it takes wing, it becomes a bird.
Unequal to hard tasks of the state,
I am again in a narrow strait.

我真的要警惕,防止这后患。

没人派蜂蜇我,我自求刺痛之苦。

开始时是小小的鹪鹩,飞起来就是个大鸟。

不堪家中多难,我又碰上这么多倒霉事。

　　此诗像是君王罪己之作。"小毖",应是小心谨慎之意。亦适用于普通人,稍不小心,便让祸患作大,自求其苦。此诗旨在成王隐威自省,寓毖后于惩前,其实正是对群臣的威慑。"惩前毖后"这一成语即由此诗而来。

①肇允:开始。②桃虫:鹪鹩,一种小鸟。

闵予小子之什·载芟

载芟载柞(shān)，其耕泽泽。千耦其耘，徂隰徂畛。侯主侯伯，侯亚侯旅，侯彊侯以。有嗿其馌，思媚其妇，有依其士。有略其耜，俶载南亩，播厥百谷。实函斯活，驿驿其达。有厌其杰，厌厌其苗，绵绵其麃。载获济济，有实其积，万亿及秭。为酒为醴，烝畀祖妣，以洽百礼。有飶其香，邦家之光。有椒其馨，胡考之宁。匪且有且，匪今斯今，振古如兹。

Cultivation of the Ground

The grass and bushes cleared away,
The ground is ploughed at break of day.
A thousand pairs weed, hoe in hand;
They toil in old or new-tilled land.
The master comes with all his sons,
The older and the younger ones.
They are all strong and stout;
At noon they take meals out.

They love their women fair.
Who take of them good care.
With the sharp plough they wield,
They break the southern field.
All kinds of grain they sow
Burst into life and grow,
Young shoots without end rise;
The longest strike the eyes.

The grain grows lush here and there;
The toilers weed with care.
The reapers come around;
The grain's piled up aground.
There're millions of stacks fine
To be made food or wine.
For our ancestors' shrine
And for the rites divine.

The delicious food
Is glory of kinghood.
The fragrant wine, behold!
Gives comfort to the old.
We reap not only here
But always in good cheer.
We reap not only for today
But always in our fathers' way.

拔掉杂草砍掉树,耕地肥沃。

众人齐齐耕耘,从湿地到田畦。

劳动者有那家长与长子,那叔叔和众兄弟,那家中壮男和普通伙计。

休息时吃饭呼呼有声,瞥见美丽妇人,还有强壮男子。

磨快犁头,开始耕种南亩,播下百谷。

种子被覆盖,然后开始生长,幼苗长得茁壮。

壮苗美好,这一大片苗儿都多么美好,除草时动作要绵软。

收获丰盛,粮食露天堆放,万亿数量难计量。

酿成清酒与甜酒,先给祖宗献上,祭礼多种多样。

食物之香,邦国有光。

美酒之馨,让老人更健康。

不仅这里这样,不仅今天这样,自古如斯。

此诗是周王在秋收后用新谷祭祀宗庙时所唱的乐歌。祭祀是一年劳作的总结,这首诗回顾了这一年从春耕到秋收的全过程,是对祖宗的汇报,也是对自己这一年的肯定与鼓励。此诗有助于研究西周社会形态,了解农业生产力的发展,具有重要的史料价值。

①厌:美好。

闵予小子之什·良耜

畟畟良耜,俶载南亩。播厥百谷,实函斯活。或来瞻女,载筐及筥,其饟伊黍。

其笠伊纠,其镈斯赵,以薅荼蓼。荼蓼朽止,黍稷茂止。获之挃挃,积之栗栗。

其崇如墉,其比如栉。以开百室,百室盈止,妇子宁止。杀时犉牡,有捄其角。

以似以续,续古之人。

Hymn of Thanksgiving

Sharp are plough-shares we wield;
We plough the southern field.
All kinds of grain we sow
Burst into life and grow.
Our wives come to the ground
With baskets square and round
Of millet and steamed bread.

With straw-hat on the head.
We weed with hoe in hand
On the dry and wet land.
When weeds fall in decay,
Luxuriant millets sway.
When millets rustling fall,
We reap and pile them up all.

High and thick as a wall.
Like comb teeth stacks are close;
Stores are opened in rows.
Wives and children repose
When all the stores are full.
We kill a tawny bull,
Whose horns crooked appear.
We follow fathers dear
To perform rites with cheer.

磨利这犁头,开始耕耘南亩。

播下那百谷,种子被覆盖后生长。

有人来看你,背着筐与筥,黍饭飘香。

草编的斗笠,锄头锋利,除去杂草。

杂草腐烂,黍稷茂盛。

镰刀响挃挃,收获何其多。

粮食垛子像城墙,排得整整齐齐。

粮仓全部开启,粮仓全部装满,女人与小孩都安心。

杀了这个公牛,牛角又弯又长。

延续过去的规矩,像先辈那样祭祀。

此诗是周王在秋收后用新谷祭祀宗庙时所唱的乐歌。祭祀是一年劳作的总结，这首诗回顾了这一年从春耕到秋收的全过程，是对祖宗的汇报，也是对自己这一年的肯定与鼓励。此诗有助于研究西周社会形态，了解农业生产力的发展，具有重要的史料价值。

①伊黍：炎帝在黎城发现嘉禾，冠以其父之名，叫作伊黍。

第六章

于胥 × 乐兮

CHAPTER SIX
In happiness
they are drowned

驷之什·驷

驷驷牡马,在坰之野。薄言驷者,有驈(yù)有皇。有骊有黄,以车彭彭。思无疆,思马斯臧。

驷驷牡马,在坰之野。薄言驷者,有骓有駓,有骍有骐,以车伾伾。思无期,思马斯才。

驷驷牡马,在坰之野。溥言驷者,有驒(tuó)有骆,有骝(liú)有雒,以车绎绎。思无斁,思马斯作。

驷驷牡马,在坰之野。薄言驷者,有骃有騢(xiá),有驔(diàn)有鱼,以车祛祛。思无邪,思马斯徂。

Horses

How sleek and large the horses are
Upon the plain of borders far!
What color are these horses bright?
Some black and white, some yellow light,
Some are pure black, others are bay.
What splendid chariot steeds are they!
The Duke of Lu has clear fore-sight:
He has prepared his steeds to fight.

How sleek and large the horses are
Upon the plain of borders far!
What color are these horses bright?
Some piebald, others green and white;
Some brownish red, others dapple grey.
What fiery chariot steeds are they!
The Duke of Lu has good fore-sight:
He will employ his steeds in fight.

How sleek and large the horses are
Upon the plain of borders far!
What color are these steeds well trained?
Some flecked, some white and black-maned,
Some black and white-maned, others red.
They are chariot horses well-bred.
The Duke of Lu has fine fore-sight:
He has bred and trained his steeds to fight.

How sleek and large the horses are
Upon the plain of borders far!
What color are these horses bright?
Some cream-like, others red and white;
Some white-legged, others fishlike eyed.
They drive war chariots side by side.
The Duke of Lu has grand fore-sight:
He will drive his brave steeds to fight.

马匹健壮,在遥远牧野。

那些好马,有的黑马白胯,

有的黄中带白,有的全黑,有的红白相间,拉起车子稳如山。

直到无穷远,这马匹多么好。

马匹健壮,在遥远牧野。

那些好马,有的灰白,有的黄白,有的赤黄,有的青黑,拉起车来强有力。

永不止息,这马匹多么壮。

马匹健壮,在遥远牧野。

那些好马,有的青毛黑斑纹,有的黑鬣黑尾白,有的赤身长黑鬣,有的白皮镶黑鬣,拉起车来疾如电。

永远不厌倦,这些马匹多欢实。

马匹健壮,在遥远牧野。

那些好马,有的浅黑带白毛,有的赤白混杂,有的黑色长黄背,有的眼眶有白圈,拉起车子身强健。

脚步在中间,这些马匹脚力健。

马儿身上总有着莫名的力量感，这些好马在一起，更是生机勃勃，诗人仔细观察它们外表与仪态，写出了文字版的百马图。关于此诗的主题与作者，历来有不同看法。综合认为，这首诗写鲁国马匹繁多、鲁僖公重视马政，就是颂扬鲁国的强大。此诗以马喻人，比喻鲁国培育人才之盛。

驷之什·有驷

有驷有驷,驷彼乘黄。夙夜在公,在公明明。振振鹭,鹭于下。鼓咽咽,

醉言舞。于胥乐兮!

有驷有驷,驷彼乘牡。夙夜在公,在公饮酒。振振鹭,鹭于飞。鼓咽咽,

醉言归。于胥乐兮!

有驷有驷,驷彼乘驈。夙夜在公,在公载燕。自今以始,岁其有。君子有

穀,诒孙子。于胥乐兮!

The Ducal Feast

Sleek and strong, sleek and strong,
Four brown steeds come along.
The officers are wise,
Stay late but early rise.
Like egrets white
Dancers alight.
The drums resound;
Tipsy, they dance aground
In happiness they are drowned.

Sleek and strong, sleek and strong,
Four stallions come along.
The officers drink wine;
Early and late they are fine.
Like egrets white
Dancers in flight.
The drums resound;
Drunk, they go round;
In happiness they are drowned.

Sleek and strong, sleek and strong,
Four grey steeds come along.
The officers eat food
Early and late they are good.
From now and here,
Abundant be each year!
The duke has well done,
So will his son and grandson,
They will be happy everyone.

壮哉壮哉,四匹健壮黄马在拉车。

从早到晚忙公事,勤勉努力都为公。

鹭鸟群飞,鹭鸟落下,鼓声咽咽,醉而舞。

哎,大家都多么快乐。

壮哉壮哉,四匹健壮公马在拉车。

从早到晚忙公事,为公事饮酒。

鹭鸟群飞,鹭鸟落下。

鼓声咽咽,醉而归。

哎,大家都多么开心。

壮哉壮哉,四匹健壮铁色马在拉车。

从早到晚忙公事,为公事参加宴会。

从今开始,岁岁丰收。

君子有福,留给子孙。

哎,大家都多么欢愉。

据说，这首诗是赞美鲁僖公为国事操劳。然而，今天看起来不无讽刺，诗中人自称早晚忙公事，但似乎更忙于喝酒跳舞，很像当今社会里自称为了家庭在外浪游不归的人。

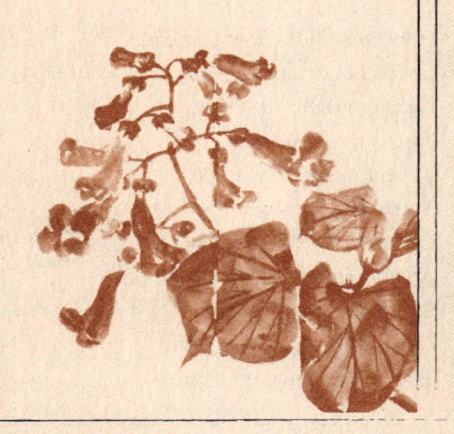

商颂·那

猗与那与！置我鞉(táo)鼓。奏鼓简简，衎我烈祖。
汤孙奏假，绥我思成。鞉鼓渊渊，嘒嘒管声。
既和且平，依我磬声。於赫汤孙！穆穆厥声。
庸鼓有斁，万舞有奕。我有嘉客，亦不夷怿。
自古在昔，先民有作。温恭朝夕，执事有恪，
顾予烝尝，汤孙之将。

Hymn to King Tang

How splendid! How complete!
Let us put drums in place.
Listen to their loud beat,
Ancestor of our race.
Your descendants invite
Your spirit to alight
By resounding drumbeat
And by flute's music sweet.
In harmony with them
Chimes the sonorous gem.
The descendants with cheer
Listen to music bright.
Bells and drums fill the ear
And dancers seem in flight.
Our visitors appear
Also full of delight.
Our sires since olden days
Showed us the proper ways.
To be meek and polite
And mild from morn to night.
May you accept the rite
Your filial grandson pays!

何其辉煌！何其宏大！竖起我的鞉鼓。

敲击出鼓声简简，取悦列祖列宗。

商汤祭祀祈祷，请赐我成功。

鞉鼓响渊渊，管声响嘒嘒。

和乐平美，循着我的磬声。

啊呀汤孙，他的时代之声庄严雍容。

大鼓洪亮，万舞煌煌。

我有嘉客，不亦乐乎。

遥想远古，先民做出榜样。

温恭朝暮，祭祀虔敬真诚。

请光顾这场祭享吧，汤孙之献。

《那》和后面那首《烈祖》一样，都是祭祀成汤。这首诗比较突出的是击鼓起舞的场面，体现了当时的礼乐之盛。

商颂·烈祖

嗟嗟烈祖！有秩斯祜。申锡无疆，及尔斯所。
既载清酤，赉我思成①。亦有和羹，既戒既平。
鬷假无言，时靡有争。绥我眉寿，黄耇无疆。
约軝错衡，八鸾鸧鸧。以假以享，我受命溥将。
自天降康，丰年穰穰。来假来飨，降福无疆。
顾予烝尝，汤孙之将。

Hymn to Ancestor

Ah! Ah! Ancestor dear,
Shower down blessings here.
Let your blessings descend
On your sons Without end.
Our wine is clear and sweet.
Make our happiness complete.
Our soup is tempered well,
Good in flavor and smell.
We pray but silently:
Bless us with longevity,
White hair and wrinkled brow.
We have no contention now.
In cars with wheels leather-bound,
At eight bells' tinkling sound,
The princes come to pray
We might be blessed for aye.
O give us far and near
Rich harvest year by year!
O ancestor, alight!
May you accept the rite
Your filial grandsons pay
And bless us as we pray!

了不起的先祖，您给我们这齐天洪福。

您给我们的恩赐无穷尽，到达所有角落。

呈上清酒，请赐我成功。

还有这调好的羹汤，它兼具五味，但又口味适中。

默默地向您祈祷，我不与世人相争。

请赐我长寿，赐我时日永久。

皮革装饰车毂，横木描画出花纹，八只鸾铃响锵锵。

请来到这里享用这一切，我受天命如此之长。

康乐从天而降，丰年粮食满仓。

来品尝我的祭品，请降福无疆。

请光顾这场秋冬之祭吧，汤孙之献。

这首祭祀成汤之诗相对而言比较平和，通过祭祀烈祖，强调无争，祈求福禄长寿，表明了很强的功利目的。

①赉：赐。

商颂·玄鸟

天命玄鸟,降而生商,宅殷土芒芒。古帝命武汤,正域彼四方。

方命厥后,奄有九有。商之先后,受命不殆,在武丁孙子。武丁孙子,

武王靡不胜。

龙旂十乘,大糦是承。邦畿千里,维民所止,肇域彼四海。

四海来假,来假祁祁。景员维河。殷受命咸宜,百禄是何。

The Swallow

Heaven sent Swallow down
To give birth to the sire
Of Shang who wore the crown
Of land of Yin entire.
God ordered Martial Tang,
To conquer four frontiers.

To appoint lords of Shang
To rule over nine spheres.
The forefathers of Shang
Reigned by Heaven's decree.
King Wu Ding, descendant of Tang.
Now rules overland and sea.
Wu Ding is a martial king,
Victor second to none.

Ten dragon chariots bring
Sacrifice on the run.
His land extends a thousand lis
Where people live and rest.
He reigns as far as the four seas;

Lords come from east and west.
They gather at the capital
To pay homage in numbers great.
O good Heaven, bless all
The kings of the Yin State!

老天命令玄鸟，降落凡间，让简狄吞下鸟蛋生契建立商朝。

住在殷地土地广阔。

上帝命令成汤，征服管理四方。

为君主号令天下，拥有九州。

商之先君，受天命而不殆，直至武丁孙子。

武丁孙子，这位武王无所不胜。

十辆马车插龙旗，酒食如山来进献。

领土直至千里，人民安居此地，统治四海之内。

四海之内俱来朝拜，来朝拜的人人山人海。

景山周围有大河，殷商受命最合宜，百禄都落到它头上。

此诗是殷商后代宋国祭祀其祖先武丁的乐歌。《毛诗序》称,《玄鸟》,祀高宗也。高宗就是诗中的殷王"武丁"。诗中先说他的家族来历非凡,后盛赞他的统治,让四海宾服。此诗成功地运用了对比、顶真、叠字等修辞手法,结构严谨,脉络清晰,气势雄壮。

图书在版编目（CIP）数据

山有扶苏：美得窒息的诗经：汉英对照/许渊冲译；
闫红解析. -- 武汉：长江文艺出版社，2024.2
ISBN 978-7-5702-3295-6

Ⅰ.①山… Ⅱ.①许…②闫… Ⅲ.①《诗经》-诗集-
汉、英 Ⅳ.①I222.2

中国国家版本馆CIP数据核字(2023)第138957号

山有扶苏：美得窒息的诗经：汉英对照
SHANYOUFUSU：MEI DE ZHIXI DE SHIJING：HANYING DUIZHAO

责任编辑：栾　喜	责任校对：韩　雨
封面设计：棱角视觉	责任印制：张　涛

出版：长江出版传媒　长江文艺出版社
地址：武汉市雄楚大街268号　　　邮编：430070
发行：长江文艺出版社
　　　北京时代华语国际传媒股份有限公司　（电话：010-83670231）
http：//www.cjlap.com
印刷：三河市宏图印务有限公司

开本：787毫米×1092毫米　1/32　　印张：10.75
版次：2024年2月第1版　　　　　　2024年2月第1次印刷
字数：135千字

定价：49.80元

版权所有，盗版必究
（图书如出现印装质量问题，请联系 010-83670231 进行调换）